I0452073

DEDICATION

The Child of my heart, Vesper Woolf...I will love you through Eternity, and then there will only be us.

For Brian Geislinger - one lifetime is not enough.

Lastly, CatFancy Magazine - a constant in my life. Seriously, I began reading this magazine in the fifth grade. "Head butts."

CONTENTS

ACKNOWLEDGMENTS

Firstly, I must give a curtsey to H. P. Lovecraft. Virtually unrecognized and misunderstood in his time, he is still the object of ridicule and his legacy maligned by academics today. Politically correct English majors amuse themselves by throwing stones at a dead man from another era. Lovecraft is a product of his time, his experiences, and the situation of his birth/childhood, as are we all.

Unlike many Lovecraft's fans today, I do not agree that he is the "father of modern horror" as Lovecraft did not write nasty, sensationalized scenes of violence and the profane such as the horror genre often depicts. To me, Lovecraft is the father of the modern dark fairytale revival, or maybe I should say, "fairy godfather." As a misanthrope, a cat-lover, and an eccentric personality romanticizing the Age of Victoria, Lovecraft is a kindred spirit of mine. This collection pays homage to Lovecraft in the form of my own feminine take on the dark-side of the airy-fairy and archetypal lore.

My inspirations and re-workings are of old Celtic lore, my brand of Southern Gothic, and classic fairy tales. A quiet childhood spent largely in eastern Tennessee, was fertile ground for an awkward, introverted girl who grew to find herself the outcast of a family simply because she craved an education and was drawn to the rich and strange. The darkest side of the Southern Gothic emerges from exposure to relatives from Alabama and the prototypical, Southern, patriarchal culture.

Gratitude goes to my husband, to whom I gave his first omnibus of Lovecraft's stories. Brian's help has been integral to the organization and publication of this collection. Without his love and support, I would not have collected my own dark fairy tales – some old, some new – to publish in this new collection.

MY SWAN PRINCE

This is a true story - but you won't believe it simply because ordinary people in an ordinary world don't believe in magic or even the possibility of it. My personal account of magical realism was the summer after my college graduation. This was when the timing was wrong for everything. The year of the Scorpio usually forecasts such. The economy sucked, people were constantly looking over their shoulders, and there was an overall oppressive feeling to the air that everything you know might just cave in around you. Everything will sooner or later. It is always just a matter of time.

In this little back watering hole of the South, time seemed actually languid like it should, or at least to people who pay attention to such things. I had moved back to my home state, many miles and moons away from my old university, my old life. My first job out of college was an average one and I was stuck waiting out the lull that had taken over the country. I was renting a small and worn but quaint house on the outskirts of a subdivision that had been birthed out of the 1920's. My particular little house stood in the corner of a cul de sac backed up to a woods and a swamp of a pond. The woods stretched up a big hill that expanded out onto the horizon only to reveal a wickedly scaly piece of land, scraped barren by loggers. Who knew that once upon a time that this ugly piece of eroding hillside was actually a wild, magical forest trodden by the Cherokee. All that may have been was now gone. Or so I thought.

That morning a bit of magic was brought to my attention by the quivering tail of my cat thumping against the window seal of my bedroom that had a direct view of the swampy pond. I admired it's collection of cattails, green algae scum and lily pads. In the middle of the pond sitting perfectly serene like a pillar of poured and molded ivory was a swan. He seemed to transcend his surroundings. Suddenly just because of his presence, the bitter and abused landscape of the distance was beautiful.

I crept outside though the creaking patio door and all the way to the edge of the pond in my house slippers and pjs. Kneeling on my haunches I tossed cereal I'd grabbed hastily from the kitchen counter out onto the water. The swan considered me with a sidelong gaze from one solid black eye barely turning his path my way. I sat Indian-style at the bank of the pond for a while and watched him glide back and forth in front of me, his black eyes occasionally blinking. Once he cocked his pretty head at me like my cat does when she wants something. Eventually, I got tired of sitting on the damp ground and went back inside to get ready for the day.

After stepping out of the shower, I peeked through my window. He was picking at the cereal and my cat was still thumping her tail against the windowpane probably wishing to be an outside cat at that moment. I went about the day's routine of work. That evening, a little before dusk I moved a lawn chair from the porch close to the end of the water and watched the swan preen until after twilight. The swan's all black eyes met mine after I threw cereal crumbs, vainly, hoping he would swim up right in front of me. Instead he flirted shamelessly, dipping his head at me, black eyes always playful. I was conscious of my cat's eyes transfixed on us behind my widow. Her eyes gleamed amber through the glass every time the moon passed through the clouds. I went back inside to find her sulking and washing behind her ears trying to appear as if she didn't care whether I spent my time with the swan prince instead of her.

That night I dreamed of the swan. The next morning he wasn't there but that afternoon he was. I would visit him under the willows and water oaks at the pond's edge often over the next couple of weeks. Occasionally, I would discover long white feathers on the lawn chair where I'd left it by the pond's edge. Finally, after the third week of the swan's first appearance he let me touch his neck. As my fingertips brushed over silky white fluff, I could feel him bend into meet my fingertips so slightly that I thought I'd imaged it.

So a habit had begun. Every day I visited him and he would slide up next to me, I'd stroke his feathers while those black eyes watched me. I thought about my swan friend constantly. I wondered how many strange lands he'd seen and where he would fly to for winter and if he would remember me and return again in the spring.

Summer crept into the hot sticky dog days that seem to never end and makes one wonder if life really has any true meaning at all. My new companion grew friendlier. I'd skim my toes over the water and he would nibble them playfully. I brought special bird food for him and he pecked it delicately out of my hands. One night I fell asleep outside and woke up to see a pair of black eyes looking up at me from the side of my chair.

I was not only thinking of the swan, but dreaming of him as well. Occasionally, I slept outside and my swan grew so familiar with me that he would snooze at my feet. One night my dreams took a turn. In the little piece of woods surrounded by encroaching suburbs, snotty-nosed boys, and the clumsy world of man, the surreal happened. My swan turned into a lanky elfin prince with hair as white as snow and eyes all black--no whites at all. His pointed ears scrolled up gracefully and he had a full smile with a deep laugh. The first morning after the strange dream I woke up with my swan resting on my stomach. His dainty head tucked back into his wing feather in ordinary swan fashion. I sat dazed in the lawn chair until he woke and shook his head gently then unfolded his wings to take flight. The swan settled in the center of the pond. All day I was distracted about the dream, remembering every detail from the musky smell of his hair to the sparkle his eyes make when he smiled.

After that dream, every night I slept outside under the stars. My companion would snuggle beside me on the nest of blankets. We counted the shooting stars and fireflies. Sometimes heat lightning would entertain us. The moths that fluttered around the porch lights laughed at us. Their gross little grizzly bodies clapped together eerily. As the summer grew to an end, so did their numbers and we took this as an omen. Moths are the hobgoblins of the winged world, being foretellers of endings in the way that butterflies signify beginnings.

Every night I saw him and every morning I awoke beside a swan. I had two lives now; one in the mundane world and one in the land of my dreams. We ignored the closing of summer and the snickers of the moth's wings. Constantly I thought of my swan and the thoughts soon turned to frantic worrying that soon he would be leaving, but never did I think it would be the way it happened.

Early one fall afternoon just after the leaves had started to turn, my swan wasn't at the pond. A bundle of dread grew in my gut as I glanced around the woods, hastily climbing the hill behind my house. My shoes and jeans were caught in brambles and young shrub trees snagged my hair in forewarning. I didn't care, and let the brambles tear at my legs and branches pull my hair. When I reached the top of the hill I could see the rest of the scalped landscape and a cove below that had been cleared as well. I stopped breathing when I saw the men by their trucks, tossing shotguns in the back of one and pointing at the white bundle of feathers at their feet. A primal scream tore from my throat as I scrambled and half-tumbled down the hill. It took me a second to reach him. His neck was sickly angled and dark sticky blood covered the feathers on his belly. The wings were outstretched and one warped from a human hand pulling on it. I took the entire swan into my arms as lukewarm blood spurted me. At first there was a shock of silence from the men. Then they attempted to apologize when they realized the animal was my "pet." When that didn't work, nervous laughter followed as a young hysterical woman, white-faced with mad dilated pupils, shrieked at them.

There were three of them, two relatively young and one old. They were all the kind that only understands other men like themselves. Holding my swan I growled out an ageless curse in a forgotten tongue. My voice was deep and steady now. They were flabbergasted and stone still. I spoke then so they could understand me.

> "Three by three, I call unto Thee.
> My beloved you took,
> So yours I call to take.
> I will it so, so mote it be."

For another minute, they stood dumbfounded then began swearing amongst themselves. They left glancing back at me warily. The fear in their eyes made me giddy with a weird kind of power but it did not sate my appetite for vengeance. I carried my dead swan back to our pond, tripping from my sobs. I buried the body by the pool. The next day I hiked out to the section of the hillside where trees still stood and carved runes in the trucks. The loggers stayed away for at least a few years after I'd left, or so I heard.

Time has passed in a fluid way that one hardly recognizes until it's gone. Years have passed now and I've moved a couple of times, once across the country. Sometimes I still dream about my swan but the dreams are no longer real, only hazy in the same way memories are as they age.

BEAUTY AND THE BEAST 2210

Terrified, she was hunched down on the metal floor of a dank ship bridge. It was not a particularly large ship, only a crew of fifteen, excluding herself – the only civilian. The sound of engines groaning and computers clicking too rapidly was the last thing she heard, along with the bellowing voices of the crew.

"Thrusters! Turn on the damn thrusters!" The blond man yelped as the panel beside him alighted in an electrical fire.

The short man at the helm yelled, "Entering atmosphere!" A sudden shudder ran throughout the ship knocking them all about as the shielding faltered a bit. They were descending, and that's the last any of them recalled.

Emma opened her eyes to a violet sky and a headache. She propped her weight up on one elbow and scanned her surroundings. Tim evidently had carried her off the ship. It stood ravaged thirty feet away from her. They'd escaped a band of infamous Arcionian pirates only two days ago to be sunk into the atmosphere of a planet far from their sector and marked as potentially volatile on all legitimate maps. Emma wished that she seriously had not applied for this position of translator/linguist, but it was too late for regrets.

Tim stumbled his way out of the ship and landed in a heap at the bottom of the ramp. "Not much to salvage it looks like, Commander, but I have sent a distress signal pin-pointed at home." The short, tubby man picked himself up with a groan.

Commander Webb nodded absently. He walked over to Emma and extended a hand, "Everything working?"

"Yeah, I think so."

"Whoa." A gasp escaped her as she turned to see what had Webb's attention.

It was a monster of a structure laid out in a complex fashion with turrets rising from the middle and ending in sharp points. Most of the windows were round and the architecture a mixture of sharp edges and contrasting liquid curves. It easily took up about twenty acres.

"What is it for?" she asked.

"Your guess is as good as mine. I don't like the looks of the inside though...like it's meant to be menacing." He ran a hand through his light hair.

"You've already been inside?" She was surprised. "How long....."

"You were out for a while." He glanced over at her. "Jackson and Nell are both dead. Their consoles exploded in their faces - so we're down two good pilots. Jane broke her neck climbing through the chambers attempting to restore the mainframe. John's critically injured. We left him in his bunk. The ship's shelter; we just can't start her back up."

"And the rest?" Emma was afraid to ask.

"Scout party is in there." He pointed to the ominous structure. "They're due to check back in anytime now." Emma took a few steps toward the ship. The design of it looked old and bulky compared to the artifice behind her. There was a perfectly placid pool of water a ways behind the ship. It stretched as far as the eye could see.

"That water's too still," Emma said to Webb.

"I know." He glared at the body of water.

"Can we go back into the cabin area?" she asked.

"Yeah, we managed to close off the bridge and engines area."

She turned to say something else, but she could tell that Webb's thoughts were elsewhere. She'd known and lived with these people for three months and liked them all. Fate seemed determined to see them killed yet.

She entered the ship from the ramp and saw where the doors to the bridge area had been sealed shut. Her little closet of a room was in the back. Emma entered her bunk and stepped into the small corner shower that barely worked. Her top was ripped and pants soiled. She pulled out a functional pair of black pants treated for all types of terrain along with a tank and over jacket issued by Earth Force. "I hate black." She muttered to herself as she packed her bag and headed out the door.

Emma noticed that Tim had opened the back emergency doors and was working diligently on the small transport car they had. He glanced across the small docking bay at Emma standing in the corridor threshold.

"Hey," he grunted.

"Hey yourself. You think we can all ride back to Earth in that?" Emma asked crossing her arms.

"Well, sure beats staying on this hell hole." Tim was obviously spooked.

"What do you know that I don't?" Emma was getting nervous herself.

Tim looked up at Emma. Taller than him by a good head, she stood twirling an auburn strand of hair around a thin finger.

"The Commander and I went inside that thing and it's freaky – kinda like something out of a Lovecraft story. The lighting is all either recessed or simply comes out of the walls. The odd thing is that the furniture looks alien of course, but it's like all a showcase from a certain era. And get this – it's bigger than anything we make." Tim's eyes were wide with emphasis on the last sentence. "We're getting out of here as soon as the scouting parties get back."

"Why did we need to scout the place out anyway?" Emma frowned.

"Cause we need a couple pieces for the upgrade I'm giving this baby. Normally, I'd just take something off the ship but it looks like everything's been shot to hell on her." Tim swept a thatch of brown hair out of his face and knelt back down by the shoddy space car.

Emma doubted they'd make it far at all in that thing. "Well I'm going to take in the scenery." Looking down she noticed a few splotches of blood on her boots. It was not her blood.

"Commander says to each pack a satchel of med supplies, water, food chips and all that good stuff," Tim called after her.

"Already anticipated that one," she called back, stepping outside.

The water could have been glass. Emma trekked out to its edge and touched the tip of her boot to the surface. It was water all right but barely moved at her touch. The water had an almost clear, glassy sheen; there was a sharp line where it turned almost black in the distance. The ground on the planet wasn't made up of grass but moss foliage. It crutched slightly under her boots.

She turned at the sound of Webb's voice calling her.

"Sir?" she said walking up to his side.

"The scouting parties haven't checked in and they're not responding to calls." Webb clicked on the communicator in his hand again. "Damn. It's definitely working... we've just lost them."

Emma sighed and waited for Tim to ask the question instead of her.

"What now, Commander?"

Webb looked from Tim to Emma. He brought a hand up to his forehead to wipe away beads of sweat. His aquiline features were taut with worry. "We go find them."

"What about John?"

He looked at Emma. "There's nothing else we can do for him and I think he'll be safer on the ship than in there."

"You bet," Tim commented.

"Here." Webb handed her a phaser gun along with a holster and a long buck knife. "You may need these."

Emma could see that both men already had weapons attached to their waist and hips. It was an odd combo with their benign-looking, beige uniforms. "Do we have any idea who's in there?"

"Emma, as far as we've been able to tell no one is in there. The information Earth Force has on this area is limited. It's claimed and controlled by the Fomorians. We've had only one a deadly introduction to them a generation ago. We don't even know what they look like."

"Just that they mutilated a whole supply ship," Tim added grimly.

"Shit," Emma whispered.

"Yep. That's what I'm gonna do if I see one."

Commander Webb rolled his eyes at his engineer, "No, you're going to shoot. If that doesn't work, retreat – now let's go."

The huge doors shut just as smoothly behind them as they had opened for them. They seemed to be antique woodwork but opened and closed automatically.

"We just stepped into a trap," Tim groaned.

Emma gasped. The ceiling resembled a sky, twinkling with tiny points of light. They were standing in a huge chamber with doorways branching off in each direction. The walls did emit a strange green light, as if they were only halfway turned on.

"This way." Webb pointed to the hallway stretching out in front of them. They followed the Commander down a long hall that deposited into a circular room of stairs and more doors. The stairway went up and down. Emma peered down over the balcony. It was a long drop.

Emma looked back behind them. "Look." She pointed at the tracks of mud and moss that they had made on the tile floor. "They walked in the same door as us so that means there should be tracks from them just like ours. There's not."

Tim groaned as his commander paced back into the main room and studied every inch of tile. Webb said nothing. He simply glanced at Emma and shook his head.

"Which way, Sir?" Tim inquired, working hard at keeping the edge out of his voice.

Webb trotted back over to the stairs. "I think I'd rather get stuck in an attic than down in a basement. We all stick together." With that, he started up the wide staircase. Emma followed close behind. They climbed up a couple of floors only to find the same scene. Each floor displayed an option of doors, one at each cardinal direction.

"Where do they lead to on the compass?" Webb glanced back at Emma.

"All a maze of sections and branches of the compound. There is not a definite layout or pattern to this structure. It's totally random, yet not."

"That's not good," Tim said softly from behind them.

"No, it's not," Webb sighed.

"Sir, should we not just go back outside and wait to see if anyone could have received our distress call?" Tim asked.

"So, basically you just want to go back outside and sit in that ghost of a ship and wait either for something to kill us or for us to starve?" Webb looked down at his engineer.

"Well, doesn't it beat getting mangled up?" Tim replied.

Webb glared to silence the shorter man. His eyes said something else, and then he glanced in Emma's direction.

"Am I in the dark on something?" she inquired.

Webb didn't respond; he just motioned for them to follow. They walked up one more flight of stairs then he abruptly chose a door to their left. It opened with the slightest touch of a hand into another dark, gloomy hallway.

"Shit," the engineer muttered under his breath.

Webb hesitated then stepped through the threshold. He was closely followed by Emma and Tim. The door shut as swiftly behind them as it had opened. Emma reached back and attempted to open it again but found it would not bulge.

"Locked." She smacked the door with her palm. "What is going on?"

"I don't know." Webb was already making his way down the hall.

"Well, this isn't working!" Emma held up the mini computerized compass. The mapping device had crashed.

Webb glanced back, "There's nothing we can do about it now."

Emma and Tim followed at a slower pace. They walked through halls leading into rooms and rooms leading into halls as well as up stairs and down stairs for the better part of two hours. She had maintained a detached calmness somehow, Tim was having an emotional breakdown, and Webb was growing increasingly frustrated with himself.

The structure was not just some command compound, but its own community. Within a couple of hours, they'd found plenty of laboratories, training facilities, offices and bathrooms, private quarters and recreational areas. The décor switched from functional to decadent depending on the use of the area. The oddest quality about the sprawling structure that disturbed them all - besides the lack of signs of anyone living - was the huge, "king-size" furniture. Tim grimaced. "Exactly how big are these people?!"

Emma threw her hands up and exclaimed just as they'd happened upon a huge library full of books and artifacts. "This is enough! We're getting nowhere fast."

"What do you suggest then?" Webb had given up on hiding all irritation in his voice.

"I need space." Tim collapsed into the chair beside him.

"You guy's want to split up?" Emma asked.

"What is this?! A relationship we're talkin' about here?! We're not splitting up," Webb reprimanded. They were both annoying her. Emma would rather be off by herself in this compound of the damned made from alien stone and mortar.

"Well, one thing's for sure. Their taste in décor leaves something to be desired," Tim snorted.

The library was immense. Shelves of books went stories up accompanied by landings and ladders for reaching them. Emma walked the space of the large towering room and took in the black walls and shelves of antique books from other worlds. The bindings were strange, but they were all books nonetheless. She'd prowled through them a bit, some of the words she knew of and some she didn't. The shelves were an odd colored green stone and cold to the touch.

"Looks all right to me."

He shot her a look. "Yeah, if you're into alien goth."

"There's a courtyard down there." Emma tapped on the huge circular window. She turned to the set of stairs to her right that led down to a balcony overlooking the garden.

"Let's go." Webb started towards the balcony door with Tim following close behind. Emma watched them leave. They turned back and waited but she shook her head. Webb only glared and said, "We'll be back."

Emma watched them rummage around the courtyard. Everything was just pointless now. Only three of them were left, and strolling around in a garden wasn't going to help matters. She was curious about the information that this place held. The library was the largest room they had seen yet with bookshelves extending all the way to the high vaulted ceiling. There were several floors of books to the room and she set out to explore them, stopping to pull off any interesting books and flipping through them. After a while, it occurred to her that the men had been gone longer than they should have. She didn't dare wander off by herself in this place. Maybe the others were just lost. She continued tell herself that.

Just as Emma had placed a pile of books on a table she caught a flash of a moving figure out of the corner of her eye. The books forgotten, Emma cautiously stepped over to the shelves where the tall shape had disappeared. She waded through the high bookcases in vain.

Sighing, Emma started down the stairs of the balcony and walked over to the round window. She didn't make it halfway when Tim bolted in from the courtyard. His face pale, he was bloody and disheveled. Clutching a wounded arm, he gasped, "Commander's dead!"

"What! How?" A tingly feeling arose along her spine.

"Didn't see – we got separated and I lost him. Heard the screaming and followed the sounds. He was all completely cut up." Tim gulped He collapsed on the floor. Emma knelt beside him. "Let's see your arm."

"Forget it." He didn't move.

"Tim, this isn't helping. We've got to get out of here."

"Right." The stocky man rose and walked toward the huge library doors. He stopped and turned to Emma with a quizzical look on his face.

"Did you hear that?"

"What?"

"Listen!" Tim pressed his ear against the door. He didn't have to. The shouts were louder. "It's one of the scout parties!" He then bolted out the door.

"Wait!" Emma called rushing after him. They ran down numerous halls and passageways. Tim was running like a possessed madman. She hadn't known him to have that much stamina. Twice she'd almost lost site of him completely.

"Tim! It's a trap!" Every time they seemed to reach the source of the screams, they dissipated into the distance again. He never heeded her words. Finally, she did lose him. Emma stopped in the middle of a breezeway catching her breath. She had no idea where he was or where she was for that matter. She peered back over her shoulder, down the hallway lined with ominous looking statues, their features lean and predatory. Sighing, Emma tried retracing her steps. Everything was too unfamiliar. It was as if the walls had uprooted and rearranged themselves. Emma paused to collect herself. She walked straight ahead. The only sound was her own breathing and she struggled to silence it. At every intersecting hallway and arched doorway, she expected an unseen pursuer to leap out.

The lighting grew dimmer as she reached the end of the hall. It seemed to just end, but in the threshold Emma saw that it actually looked down onto an enormous room. Her prescience kept her from stepping right out onto the balcony in haste.

Taking a deep breath, she stepped agilely out onto the balcony to peer down at the sight at the bottom.

Emma stifled a scream then a gag at the sight in front of her. What had been pieces of Tim and the others lay on tables in some type of meditated order accompanied by instruments that looked as if they were for more than just killing. Emma turned and made a mad dash back down the hallway.

It was by accident or hope that she made herself retrace her steps back to the library. She stopped outside the double doors. Her heart pounded in her ears as she opened one and peeked in. There was no one present. She stepped inside and closed the door softly behind her. The lighting had grown darker than it was earlier. She could tell that it was because the twin suns were setting outside. Emma forced herself to act. There was apparently no fast way out and the unseen predator had not revealed itself to her yet. She searched the balconies and floors of books for some information on these aliens. Earth Force had no sampling of their written language. She found it didn't help much that she was a linguist. Whenever Emma ran into a section that was unfamiliar to her, she grabbed an important looking book. Her aim was if she learned something of the Fomorians, she could better understand how to get out of the hellhole she'd found herself in. That was if she could decipher the language.

It had grown completely dark by the time Emma settled at a niche in between the bookcases; suddenly she remembered what seemed to be a grammar book of some sort that she had spotted earlier. The internal lights on the walls had kicked themselves up a notch so the entire library was shadowy but lit. She had to climb the ladder in order to reach it. She was a good seven feet from the floor when she felt something wrap itself around her ankle. Emma froze, turning she made herself look down behind her.

It was a hand too large to be human with a green tint to the skin. The hand belonged to a tall, broad man with long ears that ended in a scrolled point at the tips. The bone structure was large and angular. The creature had large orange eyes with enlarged sideways pupils, like a goat's. The last detail Emma noticed was the grin. Every tooth was pointed.

Emma's vision was blurry. She gasped as she raised a hand to her head.

"Sit up slowly." The voice was in clear, crisp English and definitely masculine. But it was too perfect.

Emma was in a small, small being small for this place, room lying on a lounge sofa. A wide table was across from her and on the other side of it a lanky Fomorian sat in a straight-backed chair. Her eyes were focusing now and she almost wished they wouldn't. The proportions of the man sitting across from her were daunting. Her eyes rested on a mechanical device small enough to hold in one hand. It sat on the table by the alien's pearlescent hand.

He followed her gaze. "A translator." She believed him, watching his lips move in a different motion than they should for the words he spoke in his low voice.

Emma forced herself to sit up right. "Are you a Fomorian? What is this place?"

The man's face didn't show any emotion but for the frowning of his brows. "I will ask questions and you answer." She noticed he was wearing a uniform of some sort. It was gray and functional but definitely military in appearance. His pitch-black hair was shaved into one long section from the widow's peak to the shoulder and streaked with silver. She returned her eyes to his and found he was studying her too. The eyes were the most disconcerting trait, too unblinking and largely hooded.

"Ask away," she offered. He cocked his head like a cat and looked at her with a steady gaze, elbows propped on the armrests of his chair and fingers intertwined.

"Who are you?" It didn't come out like a question, but a demand. He didn't blink an eye either.

"My name is Emma Harris and I'm the contracted linguist for the crew of the Endeavor."

His head straightened again. He moved like a phantom. "The Endeavor?"

"Yeah. The ship that's sitting on your front lawn."

He raised an eyebrow at her tone.

"I'm sorry... Look, we didn't necessarily plan to crash-land on your planet. I mean, who would want to. This place isn't exactly a five-star resort." Emma realized she was stammering - something she did in fits of anxiety. She dropped her head into her hand.

He was grinning slightly when she looked up. "Can I ask a question now?" He inclined his head forward and waved an arm in her direction. "Why is my head hurting?"

"You hit it on the floor when you fell." His face was motionless.

"What the hell do you mean when I fell?!" Emma glared at him.

"In the library, you fainted and fell." He was still expressionless.

Emma's eye's widened. "You pulled me down, didn't you? You didn't even bother to catch me!"

He laughed and Emma jumped. It was a deep resonating sound. "You're not a guest here. We do not 'help' anyone."

Emma crossed her arms. "I'm not exactly a solider, you know."

"Yes, we know. That's one reason you are still breathing."

"What're the other reasons? What of the others that you freaks from hell mangled?" Emma retorted crossing her arms.

"We established that you could ask one question." His voice was too serious and Emma folded her hands back in her lap. The series of questions that followed were concerning the protocols of Earth Force, which she couldn't answer because being a civilian, she didn't know much about them; then he inquired of their culture, customs, biology, etc. By the end of it, Emma was laying down on the lounge asking for a glass of water. He called for one to be brought in. A lanky young looking solider brought in a pitcher of water and tray of food and left abruptly. Emma wondered where they'd been hiding when her ship had landed, and during the crew's excursions inside.

"You eat and rest. I may let you ask questions next time." He got up and left the room without a glance back.

Emma was dumbfounded. She'd expected much worse and something told her that this wasn't their normal approach to off-worlders. Look at what had happened to the rest of the crew. She was it. Emma sat and waited.

She waited for what seemed like half a day. Emma explored the room, found a restroom to one side that she utilized. The restroom, the sofa thing she sat on, a table and the other chair and that was pretty much it. She wished to write, but her backpack had been taken from her so she sat with her legs curled up underneath her and waited.

Her head still ached. Emma curled up onto her side in a fetal position. Moving her hair over her shoulder, she closed her eyes. This made her sense of hearing all the more intense. Everything was dead silent. The entire structure was dormant. After a moment, she thought she heard the swishing of air vents, steady and rhythmic, barely present in the background. Emma drifted a little into a half sleep, listening to the sound of her own breathing mix with the other sound. When she felt eyes crawling on her she was brought back into awareness. She then recalled that there were no detectable air vents in this place.

Emma opened her eyes slowly and he was there, sitting across from her. She thought at first he was in some sort of trance, unblinking. She realized he was studying her, his large pupils impossible to read, she couldn't tell if he was looking at her eyes or her body. Until he cocked his head, she didn't realize he was leveling her gaze.

"We have come up with a solution," he stated simply.

Emma slowly rose to her elbow. "What do you mean 'a solution'?" she asked, not sure she wanted to hear the answer.

He leaned forward slightly and gave her a full smile. It may have been intended to be reassuring, but Emma grimaced slightly at the feline teeth. They were incredibly white, like bone. He reached out an arm to touch her. Emma jumped back and his large form sunk back in his chair. She realized that he did not mean to harm her, almost console her.

"We cannot let you return to your kind. You know too much about us. You may stay among us if you prove yourself capable." His eyes never flickered.

"What do you mean I can't go home? I don't wait to stay here." Emma leaned forward, her eyebrows arched in consternation.

The broad-shouldered man leaned toward her. Their faces were only a foot apart. "You have two options: end up like the rest of your companions, or conform to our society." His tone was matter-of-fact. She couldn't tell if he cared either way.

"Is that your test? To conform?" Emma's words were sharp. He moved abruptly and she moved back fast. He simply stood and she realized he that was motioning for her to do the same. He held out his hand, she took it and he'd pulled her up. "Follow me."

Emma sat on the platform in a long, sleek and sleeveless robe. Most of the Fomorians were dressed in similar attire, either wearing uniforms of some sort or stoic fabrics. Beside her he sat, his one long section of sleek hair pulled back at the nap of the neck. She could not remember if he had told her his name; much of their conversation she had forgotten. Emma would not be able to properly pronounce it if he had.

They were in the middle of the compound, elegant tables and chairs arranged for at least a couple hundred other Fomorians. Emma had discovered that this was just one village on an entire planet and this planet just one of the five homes of planets to this ancient race. She felt incredibly small.

He had told her what she had to do in order to live among the Fomorians. The dilemma was sacrifice her principles - that is what made her human, or sacrifice herself. Emma stood as tall and lithe as a reed, but felt eclipsed by the alien at her side. Their table was in the middle of the courtyard, on a diadem. There were a couple other older men at their table. Emma did not like the way that they looked at her. She took in the rest of the tall and lanky congregation. Fomorians were not a lively race. They all seemed to have the centering of an ancient yogi by their demeanor alone. When they moved it was almost too sharp. They all had greenish skin, some a dark shade like an olive and others a pearlescent seafoam. Their eyes, rectangular and tilted, were either a solid ebony or gold with a large slit of a pupil. The hair was all black except for the aging of silver or white. All, male and females alike were lean and angular with wide predatorial shoulders and long curving fingers. They are all planes and angles, Emma thought, with hooded eyes and elf ears. It was the ears that made them. Without the ears, they simply would have been alien but with those scrolled points, they were almost divine.

Extending his arms, all eyes were on them. Emma was too terrified to meet the gaze of those in front of her and too terrified to look away; she simply stood statuesque but quaking inside. Everything was too surreal for her senses. Her alien spoke in his own language that rolled like water off his tongue. She, a trained linguist, could not tell verb from noun. There was no pattern, no rhythm to his waves of words. They came in bursts and then would suddenly flow into one low tide. His hawkish profile hovered above her head and when his gaze turn downward to met hers, she felt her stomach drop. She shivered as his thick hand lay on the small of her back, his fingers intertwining with the ends of her long locks.

She held his gaze until movement began in the corner of her eye. Turning back to face the on-lookers, Emma saw what had become of the rest of the crew. Legs, arms, torsos all lay out and pre-sliced. The platters were even garnished with some type of foliage. She was too shocked to be sick and too disgusted to quake with fear. Emma refrained from glaring back up at him. She felt his warm hand pressing into her back then realized she was leaning into it and stopped herself. One platter was brought forward and placed on their table. All eyes were on Emma.

He spoke in her tongue, "This is your test." He moved in front of her to the side of the table. "Eat." He pointed to the platter with a sharp jerk of his head. Emma despised his smirk.

"What is the other option?" She demanded, tilting her chin to gaze at him narrowly. He studied her for a moment, then from out of his sleeve pulled out a long jagged blade. "This." He held open his hands.

It didn't take her but a few seconds. Even if she were to eat the remains of one of her crewmates, she could not keep it down. What kind of person would I be then? She thought. Emma did not want to know that answer. Sighing, she decided that she must never know. Turning to face her towering alien, she walked into his intensely golden gaze and open arms.

NIGHTMARE OF THE BELL WITCH

I knew I was dreaming simply because the person who accompanied me in my dream is not currently in my life. He was an acquaintance I'd made in Salem, Massachusetts a couple years back. Dustin was not shy about his rank in a certain tradition of witchcraft; in fact, he was rather proud of it. Being from a town that was more than Witch friendly, he did not have to worry about serious issues such as job security, which is something all Americans are supposedly protected from: religious intolerance or persecution. I, currently residing in Birmingham, have experienced and seen such life crushing bigotry firsthand. Nevertheless, I am what I am more honestly than any Christian I have ever known. One is typically born a Witch, not made one. And I inherited a cauldron from my great-great grandmother all to be blessed with the ethereal talents, and then cursed by birth into this bigot region of the New World. I inherited the ability to "dream-walk" from my Cherokee ancestry, which makes dreaming another life and world for me.

I had not spoken with Dustin in nearly a year, and it was weird I'd have a dream about us going to visit "The Bell Witch" land in Tennessee. Just goes to show you how some people abuse occult knowledge, like he did by walking into my astral travels. I'd heard stories of people visiting the land

and cave to steal a rock, only to receive the curse of bad luck. Never do this, please. The current owners of the property were not kindly people, or so I had been told by Dustin. But Dustin had wanted to go so badly. He'd invited me in real life, which I had declined. I'm a married woman that will not travel with another man without my husband. Furthermore, something intrinsically made me wary of this particular legend. Maybe it is the personal connection to the legend from my years of coming up in Tennessee? After all, her state is my home state.

In my dream, which many would consider a nightmare, Dustin and I banged on the screen porch door of a long veranda leading into the current looming white house built on the old Bell property, as the original house no longer stands. The house was old enough itself. Actually, Dustin was the one doing all the knocking. I hung back, too apprehensive to lead the way. I did not have a good feeling about this dream trip, as I knew I was there to mainly watch over Dustin. He'd pulled me along feeling that I'd have "some" connection to Her. I felt he'd do something stupid and being the Tennessean, I didn't want to see an acquaintance make a mistake involving "The Bell Witch."

Something in me has always empathized with this infamous character of local legend. I don't know why, but she resonates with me - not that I want a face to face encounter or any such encounter for that matter. I am respectful of the legend and have no desire to trespass on her cave. Even the land itself seems uncannily sacrosanct, as though blessed by an Ancient of old, an inheritor of the shamanism of Atlantis – the people who are the ancestors to this land – those the government began to slaughter before the ink was dry on the Constitution. I did not want to be there, not even in a dream. Looking out over the board high-grassed field to the back of us, I wistfully regretted feeling any ounce of anxiety over Dustin's fate. My vision caught the expanse of trees – the forest. And when I looked back around, my eyes met those of an old hag's, dark eyes wide-set, her face creases of wrinkles like tree bark. She was not soft or chubby at all. There was a certain broadness to her shoulders making her seem too unnaturally sturdy for her age, just as her skin was contrastingly taut for all the wrinkles that creased her face, as if it were bark on a tree. I inhaled sharply in surprise at her stark appearance and the fierce straight line of her mouth. She looked at Dustin as he introduced himself, his rank, his Tradition. But this did not impress the stewardess as it had me when I'd first met Dustin. She wore a long, dark, non-descript dress of calico cotton. It seemed to fit the history of the place. And when her eyes turned on me, I felt those eyes pierce my psyche to its core.

I introduced myself simply, stating I was along to make sure my friend did not get himself into trouble by doing something stupid, like taking a rock from the cave on her land. She appraised me, showing no inclination of her judgment. "You are a witch too." Her grave voice formed a statement, not a question. She knew without me offering the information. I did not wear all black and a large pentagram like Dustin. I offered a smile and we were invited inside. The hag led us through the long screen porch to a kitchen that connected to a den. All the furnishings were old and mismatched; the wood paneling on the walls as old as the house. She and Dustin haggled over the price of our visit. I was intrigued by how unremarkable the inside of the house looked and how disturbing this paradox was to me. This woman seemed to be eager to appear as anyone's Southern granny. My stomach tweaked with unease. I felt her eyes returning to me as though I'd never left her attention. I looked back at her as she told us the way, leading us outside to the path through the forest to the cave.

Dustin headed down the porch steps eagerly - I was just eager to be out of the house. I could still feel her presence behind me, knowing that if I turned, her gaze would be on me, not him. I followed a couple steps behind, glad that the sun was shining when usually I'd be lamenting about having to wear so much sunscreen. We crossed the field and into the woods where the sun shined brilliantly through the treetops, almost too preternaturally so, as though there was a little sun right underneath the canopy of branches. Then I remembered that I was dreaming. But I stayed, still confused as to why I was dreaming this dream. Was Dustin really thinking about visiting the Witch's land in person again? He'd been denied access before because the cave had flooded the year downtown Nashville was underwater.

This time he was just as unhappy when I insisted we turn around. The air, literally the atmosphere over the patch of forest ahead of us, was a black contrast to the sun streaming in overhead, the density of trees being no more so as to make such a stark contrast. I argued with him briefly; he agreed to return to the house and consult the current owner. I sighed, relieved, hurriedly leading the way back to the field.

We knocked and knocked, returning to the porch. Dustin opened the screen door and walked right back into the kitchen. I could tell he was peeved at me. We found her sitting in the den staring off into space, but when the old woman's gaze found us, she was fully cognizant. She narrowed her eyes as Dustin demanded a refund in his rude, insistent Northern way, stating he deserved his fee back since I refused to go into the dark part of the forest. I explained aloud that I would not intrude upon what is not meant for man, telling Dustin just to forget the money. It had been my call that turned us back. The hag did something unexpected; she invited us to tea, primarily me. Looking at me, she acted unnaturally gentle, as if she had to strain her voice to be so inviting. And I noticed her dark eyes turning slightly redder, like a rogue Sidhe's, as she spoke. She wanted to speak to me – I could feel her frantic urgency to keep me there. I dared not look at Dustin, though I gathered he felt the same instinct I did. We were in the presence of a most supernatural being, a creature you do not mess with, yet I knew her so well somehow.

"We can't..." I spilled excuses, "I must return to my family in Alabama. My husband misses me."

Dustin and I moved toward the doorway, to the kitchen, as her eyes narrowed. They were that rodent red, yet large in pupils and resembling a human's. This old woman was quite a bit taller than me, her back ramrod straight like a tree. And I am a tall lady. I began to back through the kitchen, offering excuses to her as she seethed, clenching her teeth with open lips in a very inhuman manner. That's when we begin to sprint through the kitchen, as The Bell Witch tore through the den. She was throwing stuff and shouting to herself, to us. Dustin surpassed me on the porch, as I screamed at him to hold the door open for me. As though it was a last minute afterthought, he actually did. My legs were heavy as though I were running through water; I could feel her at my back coming through the kitchen onto the porch.

Dustin pulled me through the door; I did not look back as we ran through the field. I knew she was right behind us as I passed Dustin, speed finally returning to my limbs. She began to call out my name beseechingly, her voice pleading with me as a female to a female. She was apologizing for her temperament in a manner. I turned around to face a breath-taking, yet astounding form of either a hybrid alien or Pre-Raphaelite beauty. Her hair was no longer bound in an iron bun, yet a long and cascading nut brown mane; her gown shimmered chiffon of dusky blues and purples with sleeves bellowing in the breeze. But her water blue eyes stayed wide set with large irises and pupils. Her eyes contained no human emotion I could decipher, and they were as clear as the sky on a midsummer's day. I wanted to console her, but feared this Being. Dustin stuck out his arm, placing it between the dryad and myself. He dared not to look as if afraid he would be enchanted by her charm. His arm kept her from coming closer to me, or so he thought. She could have grabbed me if she'd wanted to. It was as if she moved to embrace me.

Again, I told her I would not stay. I could not stay finally understanding the nature of this dream. Dustin had somehow tapped into my sleep and dragged me here, in an astral sense. He knew I am too much of a protector to let a friend be harmed. Turned out, Dustin is no friend. At first, I understood her to be a dangerous entity to us. But she didn't seem to want to harm me, just Dustin. Her rage had been directed at him for dragging me through the astral planes. However, there was a message she felt compelled to give me.

Nevertheless, I was too uneasy. As I walked backwards with Dustin's arm still between us, this gorgeous creature looked at me curiously without malice and stated in her own wonderment: "But you came right to me...."

"Was the forest not bright enough?" She peered down at me.

"You came right to me."

I awoke around three 'o clock, my feet dangling off the bed after something firmly pulled them. My husband's breathing was steady beside me; my cat dozed over my head. It was then I noticed a tall, darkly amorphous shadow slide out of our reality, right out our bedroom window.

I went back to sleep, continuing to have odd dreams. However, none of my dreams stuck with me like the one containing the dryad. Was she a dryad, a forest fey of The Ancients with the talents of a siren or gorgon? That's the mysterious origin of "The Bell Witch?" Where exactly had I been pulled to by someone who turned out not to be a friend at all? Her words played in my head the next day. "But you came right to me." Did I?

THE FELINE FACTOR

Oh, bewareful of those Margotine Cats from Brittany!" the old, smelly false mothers would moan. They made sure to adequately scare all the young girls especially, so as to ensure that they would grow up to be obedient spouses to their self-opined spotless sons. In this particular village, Cats are considered bad fortune. For They – these Catmen of a foreign shore – lead astray pretty, little things from the village, the land of church, the men, and a god that is jealous.

Once upon a time, not so long ago at all...there was a beautiful young woman with auburn hair that danced around her waist and legs, which were so long that prancing fawns even envied her. Allison had not been long in her young womanhood when she followed the grinning cat into the forest, through the grove and into that rusty gate adjoined to a wrecked stone wall. Only a rolling landscape full of rocky cairns occupied the space beyond the gate with a rolling sea in the distance, as a singing neighbor. Allison had never ventured beyond the rusty gate; she'd not dared to open it – for the elders claimed it was a portal to a bad, horrid place, particularly for curious, pretty young girls. Why girls like Allison were expected to breed more pretty little babies! Then conventional wisdom would gobble up another generation of delicate, young minds. The funny thing about conventional wisdom is that it is not wise. In fact, Allison knew in truth, it's really just a bundle of conventional lies.

Allison, pure of heart and soul, knew that there were more sides to creation than what she had been taught. She did not absorb the embittered rants of the old village women, whose bodies were as rusty as this gate from societal demands and overuse. Allison did not pay attention to the boys who called out her name, trying in vain to distract her from her path. She knew what they wanted; she'd seen what happened to other beautiful, both wed and unwed girls who allowed themselves to be ensnared by a deceitful man.

Allison left the village one fine morning with a meager bag of her possessions, wearing a pair of witchy black boots on her feet and ivory lace dress on her body. She had remembered to pack a lunch, not knowing if she'd stop at the market or not, she didn't – she found the grinning cat right away – or he found her.

Prancing about the bricked streets of the village square, the tabby cat wove in and out of unsuspecting legs. Men yelled: "A cat! A Cat! It's old Luc for sure!" The matrons belted: "Allison! Do not look – turn away from temptation." And when Allison heeded none of their calls and warnings, they blasted accusations at her: "Selfish little witch!" "Who does she think she is?" "How dare she think her life exists for herself?!" "Witch!"

Their words melted like snowflakes before ever reaching Allison's ears. She couldn't have heard them – Allison was too busy running after a large, grinning tabby. She ran straight out the town gates without so much as a thought to glance back over her shoulder. She stopped at the iron gate, rusty from sea air. She gave it a little shove with a wink from the Margotine tabby. As she steps through the threshold, Allison's world shifts. She finds herself no longer just a young woman from a provincial village.

Allison blinks several times before she decides that the edifice in front of her is real. It's a huge sand castle – twice as large as any castle she's ever seen before. The shape of the shoreline has changed. The waves now crash in a clapping rhythm against the foundation of Welsh blue stone, hammered cliffs of salt water that stretch along the coastline as far as Allison can see. And all the cairns have grown into miniature lighthouses dotting the rolling hills. Allison does not even look back to shut the gate. She knows it will not be there. She's entered another realm.

And that grinning cat is nowhere to be seen! "Mr. Cat? Oh, Mr. Cat…." Allison cries in vain, but no one responds. She sets her sight on the sand castle of giants and begins to wade through a sea of bluish grass. The occasional lighthouse she passes is manned by ferrets complete with sailor hats and telescopes. One gray ferret waves Allison over. She sighs, not wanting a distraction on her journey, but compiles.

"And who ye be, Missy?" the ferret inquires, craning his neck to look at her from the balcony of the lighthouse. The ferret finds himself eye level with Allison.

"Why, I'm just a young woman looking for a better life," Allison answers quizzically, surprising herself with the honesty of her answer.

"And does this young woman have a name?" The ferret removes his eye patch to study her with two perfectly healthy eyes.

"I'm Allison." The girl curtsies, amused.

The ferret salutes her: "And I am the lighthouse keeper – *your* lighthouse keeper to be exact."

"Oh, how delightful to have my own lighthouse keeper!" Allison exclaims as she clasps her hands together.

"Yes, how very neato, indeed!" The ferret pulls himself up to stand on his hind legs, arms akimbo.

"Tell me, dear Keeper, whose sand castle is that?" Allison points to the castle glittering in the sun from all the sand particles that form its massive walls.

"Oh, darling, that's not sand at all – it's stardust," the ferret replies, shaking his head. "You must be from a very provincial place."

"Yes, I was. But no longer am now." Allison wrinkles her nose at the fleeting brief memory of her old village. "Stardust." The word rolls off her tongue in an audible whisper.

"Oh, yes darling. Stardust – the building blocks of life," the ferret explains. Allison turns to leave as the keeper cries: "Wait! You're forgetting something!"

"Oh, how rude of me! Goodbye!" She taps the ferret on the head with a gentle finger tip.

"No! Not that – though the afterthought was kind despite being an afterthought and all..." Huffing, the Keeper extends an open paw. "Here."

"A seed?" Allison is confused.

"Oh, it's not just any seed, silly girl! It's a star seed – a seed of inspiration!"

"Hmmm." Allison, curious, allows the Keeper to drop in her hand."

"You'll know what to do with it when the time comes. Now go....Go!" The Keeper waves and Allison is off, wading through the sea of grass.

"Hey, watch where you sit those things!" a grumpy, hissing voice spouts from below. Startled, Allison jumps back. It's a snake! A pretty black snake with twinkling blue eyes.

"Pardon me!" apologizes Allison, who begins to stammer further apologies when the snake shouts: "Stop! Enough already! I'm just your guide!"

"Oh," Allison mutters. "How very interesting..."

"Why yes, it is, isn't it?" retorts the snake.

"Follow me and I'll lead you to the right door," she assures Allison.

"Sure, how kind of you – but who lives here?" Allison replies. The snake hisses in agitation. "Why don't you already know?" Allison huffs: "How could I know when I've never been here before?"

"Just because you don't remember it doesn't mean you haven't been here before," the lovely snake responds cryptically. "And you do know who owns the castle."

Allison can get no further answers from the snake, who occupies the rest of their journey by singing Mother Goose rhythms all wrong. She inquires how her Guide knows who Mother Goose is, but she slithers on without answering:

"Hey doodle, diddle,
The Cat and the pickle,
The dog was kicked right over the moon!
And the little girl laughed out of spite.
And the fish ran away with noon!"

"Excuse me! I don't think that's how it goes…" interjects Allison, but the snake continues only to slither quicker through the grass and Allison must trot to keep up.

As they near the corner of the great castle, Allison pauses with the snake under a great oak. He is one of the only trees on the rolling fields. Leaning a hand on the rough bark, Allison startles at the fluttering and rustling above her head. A great horned owl shakes out his wings and studies her with large orange orbs.

"Whoo-hoot!" the great owl calls down. Allison stares transfixed. She's always been fond of owls, but has never been this close to one before. "Hello up there!" Allison calls. "Hello down there!" The owl responds in a deeper voice than the lighthouse ferret.

"Who are you, now?" Allison asks the owl, who laughs and asks rhetorically, "Why you've got this all figured out, don't you now? I'm your guard!" And with great gusto, the owl puffs out his chest leaping up into the air currents. He soars up and over the castle of stardust. Allison stares after him, wondering at emerging twilight. She watches as the first stars pop out of the night sky. The cerulean blue shifts to dark lavender and at the very corners murky shades of sapphire, as dusk emerge.

"You do want to make it inside by nightfall, don't you?" the snake calls as she slithers on. Allison trots behind her and as they approach the castle, she discovers that it's too high for her to crane her neck and see the very top from this vantage point. And there's more than one main entrance; many doors with there own staircases, all different shapes. Some doors are ornate, some arched, some French, and some rather plain. Allison reaches out to touch the stardust wall to discover sea shells embedded in the mortar of the castle. She taps a large nautilus and the crashing waves from the other side of the castle's foundations suddenly sound all the louder.

"Ah! This is the one!" the snake hisses as she leads Allison up a spiral staircase and through a rounded door rimmed with blue and smoky quartz. When Allison steps through the threshold, she finds herself on a landing, two twin staircases greet her – one to the left and one to the right. The stairs on the right are deep burgundy and rather worn. The staircase on the left is made of a burnished brown hardwood.

"Which one?" Allison asks the snake. But she simply slithers away and begins to fade.

"Wait! Where are you going? Don't leave me!" Allison begins to panic.

"Silly girl, I'm always with you!" And with that the snake is completely gone.

Taking a deep breath, Allison studies each staircase briefly and chooses the left one. She can tell that it reaches higher, right into the castle's turrets. "Who am I to follow what is the proverbially 'right' path anyway." Allison mutters to herself. "I claim this life for myself." And she climbs, her boots making a delicate clapping on each stair. On and on the staircase twists; Allison stays on course – not stopping to venture down a darkened hall. "I do not wish to take the time." She explains to herself. The staircase climbs to the tallest turret where Allison steps out into moonlight. She gasps at the night sky, completely sapphire with twinkles of diamond starlight winking at her across time and space. She can see the surface of the moon and the ice caps on Mars. And then across the tower's tiled floor, Allison sees him.

"Who are you?" she gasps. The orange grinning Cat is much bigger than just the size of a fox. In fact, he stands taller than Allison by a good foot. He stretches out his long legs as he leans against the tower's balconied edge; he hasn't the slightest fear – of anything. The Margotine Cat reaches a pawed hand into his double-breasted blazer and pulls out a bauble. "Remember this?" He inquires, extending a tabbied hand. In the middle of his palm rests an antique key. "Here, I've polished it up for you."

Allison walks across the towers top to the Cat's outstretched hand. His paw hand is soft and his claws are retracted. She takes the key and places it in the pocket of her lace dress.

"Don't forget and misplace it again." The towering Cat grins – his teeth completely feline. His amber eyes are upswept and large; he twitches a pointed ear and stares back at her. "You'll understand." He says simply. Allison hears an owl hooting in the night. "Where to now?" she asks. The Cat laughs, "You tell me. It's your life."

Allison stretches out an arm. Reaching inside the Cat's blazer, she wraps her arm around his waist. The waves suddenly are singing below against the castle's walls. "And you'll come with me?" The Cat leans his head close: "I've always been with you." His breath is warm and Allison relaxes. She knows that she is awake.

SNOW WHITE ON ACID

Not long ago a comfortably married couple decided to have a baby. The baby's mother did not sit beside a window looking out onto a picturesque snowy scene and prick her finger on an embroidery needle. Nevertheless, the poor girl ended up with hair as dark as a windowpane, skin as white as snow, and lips as red as blood.

"Snow White," (I'll call her that just for the story's sake), didn't really amount to much as far as self-worth is concerned. She was far from vogue as far as pigmentation and coloration went for her time. To some Snow White was a vision, if you were into the goth look. To others she was a different looking girl with a hawkish face who could have been quite attractive if only she'd streak that hair and get a nice tan.

However, she had decent parents and a subdued lower-middle class childhood filled with trick-or-treating, a couple trips to the beach, and visits from the likes of the Tooth Fairy and Easter Bunny. She was a painfully shy child, always eager to please. Everyone always remarked on how mature she seemed for her age. Snow White was so good – always wanted to be so good. She didn't go to her proms, never made all A's, and certainly wasn't popular in school. But she did win citizenship awards and certificates citing model behavior.

Babies are born egocentric and most people never seem to grow out of that disposition. Snow White never lived with the illusion of a perfect universe revolving around her. She had the unfortunate other extreme of putting everyone above herself and, therefore, always felt belittled and used. She was after all known for her infinite kindness much like the image all little Catholic girls are told to strive for: "The Blessed Mother". So what's a good girl to do?

Snow White started college like too few of her peers. She concentrated on her studies mostly; not being especially bright, she had to. She did acquire a close little circle of friends who all thought she was just too sweet. She was the one to have copies of typed notes for you if you missed a class or two. She was the one to buy your lunch if you happened not to have lunch money. Sometimes they remembered her kindness but mostly it went unnoticed as good things always do.

One day Snow White was sitting with a couple girl friends in the foyer of the Humanities building when a clumsily tall guy approached. He had an odd shaped face that only some designer in the modeling world would find attractive. Snow White was not one to judge, only observe, or so she thought at this time in her life. He swayed when he walked as if he was proud of his stature, but didn't know how to carry the height at all. He had a quirky smile that tugged almost vulgarly at the corner of his lips when his eyes focused on someone, and that someone at this moment was

Snow White. He took the liberty of sitting down beside the girls - without asking - right beside Snow White. The expression on her face must have been quizzical as he extended his hand in greeting. His name is not important just like Snow White's real name isn't, so we'll just call him Demon.

Demon introduced himself to all three girls. He was a couple years older than Snow White and currently studying some odd art movement she'd never heard of and probably wouldn't have an impact on world history when it outlasted its phase. They listened politely to what he had to say then discovered Demon was in their history class. He was usually absent, due to devoting so much time to his art creations. He had seen Snow White pass a smoothly typed sheet of notes to one of the girls and asked if he could have one. They gave him an extra one expecting him to leave, but he didn't.

He didn't care that he had interrupted the study group. Demon was now only interested in Snow White, and she didn't have much to say to guys in particular. If he noticed their discomfort, he ignored it and kept running his mouth about things no one really had an interest in. "I'm a Renaissance man." He stated and they exchanged confused glances. When the bell rang, he left and they went to class remarking on what an odd character he seemed. Snow White didn't give the guy who couldn't carry his height much thought after that.

A couple days later, she would see him again in the halls. He was walking aimlessly as if in an alternate reality no one had the ability to see but himself.

Demon saw her and waved immediately heading her way. He thanked her for the notes and inquired if she'd looked into the art he'd told her about. She replied she'd just been too busy with her studies. He seemed slightly agitated at this and reiterated how important it was. "Art is the window to the soul." He motioned with his hands and swayed slightly as if trying to catch his balance. Demon had heard the phrase somewhere and stored it in what little memory banks he had for future reference to impress a girl. It didn't impress Snow White but rather made her feel sorry for him. He was so odd that he probably had few friends. He came across as one of those former dorks who are always bullied in school. She listened to his lecture about some other kind of art then politely dismissed herself using the excuse she just had to get to class. Demon called excitedly after her that he'd love to explain the fundamentals of surrealism to her sometime. Snow White simply waved, thinking to herself, "what a poor pathetic soul."

He began to sit close to Snow White and her friends in history class. She was as nice to him as she would have been anyone else. He got to know a little bit about her, her life, aspirations and goals. Demon was as crafty as his pen name and knew that to reel someone in, one would have to appeal to her sensibilities. And that's exactly what he did.

"Oh, you're an environmental science major! What a calling! To strive to protect our natural resources." Snow White smiled shyly. "Well, it's not exactly as glamorous as that and I don't think we have the right to call anything 'ours.'"

Demon liked the fact that she was reserved and self-conscious but felt like she had rebuffed his praise. "So you don't own your cat? You don't own your car?" he chided. Snow White simply smiled patiently and replied, "Not in the sense you mean it... and as for a car, it's not a living thing." He simply grunted and turned away to chat with another acquaintance.

After that Snow White didn't care to talk much to Demon. He seemed on edge as though he had something to prove to everyone. But one day when she least expected it he surprised her. Snow White had been having a particularly rough morning between two pop quizzes and feeling lonely since she didn't much fit in with her new friends simply because she wasn't the party type. Demon instantly saw the downcast eyes and slow walk. Her long dark hair and stark white skin stood out this time of year when all kids were sporting tans and shorts. Snow White instead wore a long, loose skirt and knit top. She was all class and he just had to have that.

"Hello, you okay?" He asked in his most concerned voice. She glanced up and hefted her book bag to the other shoulder moving off the path and out of the way of the moving flood of students. "Oh, yes, just a bit stressed, that's all."

"Well, I'll buy your lunch today. How about the café down town?" Demon smiled boyishly. It momentarily almost reminded her of a boy she'd gone to school with. Where was he now she wondered?

"Well...." He brought Snow White out of her reverie. Austin had short white blond hair, a whole shock of it, she thought to herself. His is much too dark mousy brown and frizzy.

She studied him. He must be lonely himself. The only other people that would have anything to do with him were the weird art students.

"Are you sure?" she asked.

"Yeah, why would I have asked if I wasn't?"

"Okay then. I'll meet you down there at one thirty."

Demon grinned, "See you there!"

He watched as Snow White made her way through the crowd of young adults. So many different types of people he thought to himself. Yet everyone had someone out there. Snow White, he just knew was meant for him.

Demon watched from the window as she approached the little café nestled on the main street by oddity shops and a park across the street. Snow White had parked her old Ford on the other side of the park, walking head high toward the café taking time to let the surroundings sink in. He knew that she was new to this area. He got up and opened the door for her as she crossed the threshold.

"How quaint." Snow White smiled at the expressive café with its wildly painted walls and antique furniture.

"Told you I was a Renaissance man." Demon had that quirky grin on his lips but she ignored it.

"What do you want?" he asked as they approached the counter.

"Oh, just a vegetarian sandwich and cappuccino."

He motioned for the young guy with green hair behind the counter and made a big production of paying for Snow White's lunch. She was occupied with studying the café and its odd paintings that looked like they had been painted by three year olds. Not exactly her preferred style of décor.

"So you actually taking out a girl?" the green haired guy with lots of piercing asked.

Snow White replied, "We're friends from college. Do you go to school anywhere?"

"Used to," the bored replied from the young man behind the register sounded down-trodden. Snow White proceeded to inquire about his intricately weaving, neat body work when Demon, listening to the exchange, interjected. "Well, we may be dating. I mean I did buy your lunch."

Snow White sighed, "I've bought friends lunch before. It's cool."

They took a seat by the window and Demon seemed to be sulking. He mainly asked Snow White questions about what she thought of this and that. She answered them tritely wondering why he was so curious about her opinions on things from religion to world events.

"You're not talking as much as you usually do. What do you think about all that...that philosophical stuff you were asking me about?" she asked as the green haired guy bought their food. He clapped Demon on the shoulder. Demon acknowledged the gesture with a slight nod of the head.

He seemed busy with his food for the next few minutes then perked up. "You wanted to know what I think about such things." He was trying to sound poetic and smart. "Well, I'm a Humanist but a Christian as well. I go to The Word for my advice and opinions. Directly what it says is how I feel about the world we live in and all that is." He made a flamboyant hand gesture and looked as if he were about to fall out of his chair for a moment.

"That's nice," Snow White replied politely. She had been raised Catholic but wasn't particularly religious. He had not come off as a conservative with his art talk, unkempt hair, ripped jeans and punk jacket.

"So you're conservative on issues?'"

"Oh no, I see them as non-issues. Don't you see? There is so much more...so much feeling. Through Yahweh is true happiness and then there is no controversy."

He must have read the look of confusion on Snow White's face. "Oh you don't understand!"

Snow White answered honestly, "Why, no, I don't. Don't the Jews refer to god as Yahweh? I thought you said you were Christian?"

Demon rolled his eyes and laughed lightly. "That's what HE is called in The Word. We all are entitled to know HIM as such."

Snow White noticed the emphasis on the pronouns for his god. He was into this stuff like she was her favorite TV show. He carried on excitedly with an almost feverish enthusiasm. He ended with, "So what do you think?"

"Well, I was raised Catholic and have studied other religions but not different forms of Christianity, other than Catholicism of course. I have my own ideas based on what I've learned. And they are of a more universal perspective."

"So you rely upon worldly means of enlightenment?" Demon's voice held a hint of taunting.

"Yeah, what isn't 'worldly'? I mean nothing got beamed off the starship *Enterprise* for our reading enjoyment." Snow White let exasperation seep into her voice. "Look, I just respect everyone's right to find their own path." He seemed a nice enough guy but the conversation was beginning to be a bit too intense.

He drew himself up straight and replied, "I don't think god is anything to joke about. I'll just have to show you."

Snow White laughed for real now, "I'm out of Catholic school and no one is going to show me anything anymore."

He'd never seen her so animated, so sure of herself. "You need to be more humble." He said it softly on purpose, almost patronizingly.

Snow White looked at him critically munching on her sandwich. She wasn't sure what to think of this odd ball in front of her. His eyes were currently big and full of meaning.

"This is an odd town," she remarked out loud. And as it turned out, Chattanooga, Tennessee was an odd town.

Over the next couple months Snow White got to know Demon a bit better. She had summed up correctly that he had been a social reject in school, his mother was a corporate slut, and his father a redneck that use to beat his mother when she was still married to him. All that explained his need for his weird ideas about all that jesus and god stuff. Demon hung out with Snow White and her friends sometimes on the weekends; he grew familiar in a comical way. Some of her friends thought he was attractive in a roguish way. He was a rebel of a sort and did have almost feminine features that a lot of girls seem to like. Snow White felt sorry for him. If only he could get some issues straightened out he might be able to live up to his full potential.

Demon had also gotten to know Snow White better as well. She wasn't a frail push over as he first thought but strong in her own way. She had a remarkable ability to calm people down and brought an air of diplomacy to situations, like the other day when he nearly told off their professor for teaching evolution. She still didn't want to see The Truth the way he did and he despised her stories about her old friends, cats and home. Where the fuck was Cullman, Alabama anyway? He wanted her to see him in a supreme light. That he was better than the friend she talked of, and the guy that insisted on sitting beside her in her astronomy class. He resented the fact that she'd rather study than go out with him. He knew that she didn't see it as a relationship but rather a friendship and this disturbed his already much disturbed mind. There was a lot about himself that he wouldn't tell Snow White. He couldn't if he wanted her, wanted her purity, her talent. He seethed over how effortlessly it was for her to draw a life-like animal. She was not even an art major! She could read undisrupted for hours, while his racing thoughts interfered with his ability to concentrate on anything for too long. He had to have what she had. And then there was the lust. She was attractive, but in an odd way; almost in an old way as if she came out of another time. No, the guy who sat beside her in astronomy class wouldn't get her. Neither would the childhood friend. She would see. She would see how amazing he was and would carry him to where he wanted to be in life.

And so he adapted himself to pursuing her. He became the perfect gentleman, dressed better, acted considerately and pretended to like things she liked. He wanted to be with her constantly and pretended to be a listening ear when she wanted to talk to someone. This would allow him entry into her time, her world more. He liked the way she dressed. It was different but so flattering. She wore more skirts than most girls and was kind to everyone.

The other night he'd broken down and cried in front of her about some things he thought were particularly tragic in his childhood. It was the second time he'd done so. He just loved how she comforted him and told him everything was okay now. Then he'd had the opportunity to console her when one of her cats had died. He was the perfect companion. He took her out to eat and let her talk about the life of the animal and their history together. Demon felt they had bonded enough on a friendship level and he began to push it a bit further. He would bring her flowers and leave notes on her car. She began to soften to the idea of dating him and he seized the opportunity he'd been waiting for.

They were walking together to class one day down the main path on campus. Snow White was listening to what Demon called his "witty banter." All of the sudden he was interrupted from his lecture on the purity of Impressionism when a guy who somehow apparently knew Snow White came up and started talking to her while he was right there! Right beside her! They were discussing biology of all things. How sly of the guy to worm his way in so innocently, Demon thought to himself.

"So when's the study group meeting?" the intruder asked. He was a handsome guy with sandy hair, the All-American type.

"Tomorrow night at the library. Jesse reserved a study room for us already." Snow White smiled at him. Demon couldn't stand it any longer. He cleared his throat loudly and both looked at him.

"This is ____." Snow White spoke Demon's name.

He extended his hand, "Hello, this is my girlfriend."

Snow White looked at him again.

"Oh, yeah." The All-American Joe shook his hand, returning the grip. "What's your major? Do you two take many classes together?"

"I'm an artist," Demon replied flatly.

"He's an art major," Snow White replied for Demon, aiming to break the tension that Demon had put in the air.

"Well, nice running into you and meeting you. Take care." Joe did a quick salute and headed down the shady lane past the university's old stone buildings.

"I think he's military," Snow White began, but Demon was walking already.

"Hey, wait up. What's the matter?"

He continued to walk until they were halfway to the cafeteria then turned around and hissed, "You know damn well what's wrong! What was that back there?!"

"What are you talking about?" Snow White was astounded by his attitude and noticed that a couple people were looking their way. Demon sneered down at her as if he wanted to attract attention.

"About John! About betrayal!" His nostrils were flaring now.

"John is just a guy from my class that's in my study group. Lower you voice, people are looking," Snow White said lowly.

"Lower my voice! I don't care who hears that you're a cheating bitch! You're fucking John!" Demon had raised his voice, secretly loving the drama transpiring and Snow White's shock. She should have known better. She'd asked for this. That was his how his disturbed mind processed his jealousy.

Snow White raised her voice, but it was calm. "John is simply a guy in my class and do not cuss at me."

"Don't you play games with me! You sneaky bitch – just like other women!" Demon enjoyed his self-righteous moment, basking in the attention from on-lookers. "Do you think I deserve this? I can do so much better!" He stomped off leaving Snow White speechless and embarrassed.

Later on that evening he would leave a note and poem on her car about how sorry he was about his "artistic" temperamental outburst. It's just that the circumstances reminded him of a bad memory. He wouldn't let it happen again... and that he needed her. She made him a better person. Then he called and begged her to forgive him; that she was just so good and lovely. Of course it worked. And the next night he conveniently had a personal crisis where he needed her dear affections and she missed the study group.

Snow White just didn't know what was wrong with her. She felt like a bad person. She didn't want to hurt Demon's feelings, but she needed time and space for herself and her studies. When she told him so he would pout up and claim she was not sincere in her love. She tried to explain to him how they hadn't know each other long at all and he would gush how he felt he'd known her for ages and she was what he had always wished for. As they were sitting on the sofa in her home, Demon had asked her to rub his head where it hurt only to yell at her for not paying attention to him, claiming she was more interested in the TV. She was glad her parents were not home.

"How dare you think that a show is more important than me!" He growled pushing her away from where they sat on the floor. He was about to have another fit. It had been six months since they'd been dating and he had a fit once a week or so. Demon always apologized and was so much better afterward. He made her feel as if she was helping him work through his issues; that she owed him that much. Snow White didn't know what was happening to her, only that she was in constant doubt of herself. Her grades were dropping and she felt worn out all the time. The other week he became irate because she had not ordered fast enough at a Mexican restaurant. When he was happy he was so good and he said she brought that out in him. If only she could be patient with him at times. She had so many doubts and was on the verge of totally breaking contact with him.

Demon could sense that she was getting away. He was enraged at her independence. Didn't she see he was so right on everything? Demon would not let her get away. He would win. She owed him so much. He thought that he deserved so much in his sick perverted mind, personally entitled to anything he craved in life. He had a plan and it worked.

Six more months had passed and Snow White was convinced she was marrying the man of her dreams. No matter that there hadn't been such a concept as a man of her dreams before. Demon had fewer outburst in the past few months and contributed this to her. She had reformed his opinion of womankind.

The few tantrums he had thrown she just knew were really her fault. She should have known better than to wear that red dress to school. She'd made him jealous, he'd said. That's why he behaved the way he did and said the things he did. "I'm your prince...don't you want to please me?' He would ask when she said something he didn't agree. She was so stupid, always messing up.

Demon said he felt close to god, so she must realize that god came first. Snow White still thought some of his beliefs strange but who was she to try to change him. He on the other hand demanded her make concessions. When she asked how he rationalized that as fair, he simply stated religious beliefs were to be respected and his being the one true way certainly should. He lived for christ. Demon claimed that she and his beliefs made him good, that they kept him grounded and focused.

When Demon was good, he was so good. He had a way with winning people over and making people feel sorry for him. He was the best friend that Snow White was lacking after moving away from her home state. She came to overlook and then to ignore his faults.

The day Snow White took vows with Demon everything was too bright, too bright in the way mirages are. The hobgoblin of a minister matched the wickedly gnarly tree outside the courthouse. They were the only ones present. Later Snow White wouldn't recall anything about the farce of a service at all. Demon insisted on breaking the news to all his artist and punk friends immediately after. Snow White blushed deeply when they snorted and made vulgar jokes. She was anxious to be rid of them.

They lived in a small, old apartment that faintly smelled of an odor she could never quite place. Sometimes she thought that it must be the smell of death, later she discovered it was sulfur. Snow White cleaned it thoroughly and got defensive when Demon followed her around the house inspecting her cleaning jobs. He chided her for it too. It didn't take Snow White long to realize exactly how needy he was. Living with him there was simply no escape. He even called her at the bookstore where she worked.

Due to his constant demands, Snow White did poorly in college and had to drop out. She was either working or catering to Demon's needs. It was an endless cycle she couldn't seem to break. When she did something for herself he would reprimand her for it. "You're being so fucking selfish. What the hell do you mean you need time alone? You want me to leave? Is that it? I'll give you all the time you need then." He would stomp about and pretend to be leaving her for good. When he first started playing that card, Snow white would cry at first, but then it become routine and she knew to expect it.

Every bit of her paycheck he managed to take and keep. When Snow White would purchase something for herself he would go into a rage immediately sometimes tearing up the item or returning it. It was all about him, and Demon was going to make damn well sure she kept that in mind. Eventually, he quit his part-time job and Snow White had to work constantly just to break even. Demon went to college on a government grant since he was technically poor on paper and hailed himself as a "house-husband." His parents, who'd never really acted as parents, had given up on him a long time ago. After all, he was the product of bad genes on both sides of the family. Even though they had been initially ugly to Snow White, they were more then happy to see someone feed and shelter their starving artist loser son.

Demon floated through his classes, ate at the restaurant of his choice, and despite his self-proclaimed title of "house husband," he did none of the housework. He drove her car and called her fat, citing that as the reason she shouldn't eat lunch. Snow White grew so thin that she could put her hands underneath her ribs and hold them in her hands. Her life was a slow death, and then entered Vesper Woolf.

One chore of a day, Snow White and Demon were shopping at a rural farmer's market when a girl Snow White's age approached her with a box of kittens. The girl had intense blue eyes, the color of rain and a voice that matched.

"Would you like a kitten? I found their mother feral and pregnant. She's unfortunately passed and since I live with my parents I can't keep her babies." Snow White knew that she didn't have the money to feed a kitten and Demon did not like cats.

"Oh, I would like one very much! Just last year I lost my childhood cat, but my husband…." Demon cut her off. "I think a kitten would be a great idea!"

Snow White was shocked and pleased by his excitement. "Well, let's see…oh, the black one has the bluest eyes!" Demon picked up the whining kitten. The girl with rainy eyes was quick to say, "That one's a boy."

"No boys! If we get a boy he'll take to you and not me. Remember Freud?" Demon looked down at the girls, trying to draw himself up to his full height. The kittens were okay but the blond girl holding the box was better. However, she seemed only interested in Snow White. The slut was probably a lesbian, Demon thought to himself.

"Look at you," Snow White said lowly to a buddle of brown and gray fur splotched with marmalade orange. "A tortoise-shell tabby." The kitten's eyes were as odd as her fur shifting from amber brown to a lime green.

"She looks wild, doesn't she? Almost like a baby of a lynx," the girl said to Snow White. Snow White picked up the kitten and was greeted with a sharp cry. The girl smiled at her, "She's a little girl." She glanced up at Demon making a point not to smile at him.

Demon was growing bored and agitated that no one seemed interested in him. "What about the gray one? Is that one female?" The girl didn't even look at him when she replied, "Yes." Snow White studied the gray tabby, but the odd colored kitten in her hand stretched her paw out to touch Snow White's chin. Snow White's attention was drawn back to the buddle of fur she was holding. The kitten looked right into her eyes, and for a brief flash the cat eyes staring up at Snow White were human.

"I want this one." Snow White's voice was decisive; but, Demon didn't care because he was bored of the whole mess anyway. "Let's go then!" He grumbled, already walking through the booths of vegetables to the parking lot.

Snow White looked at the girl with odd eyes who simply smiled slightly and nodded. She started to follow Demon then turned around to inquire more about of the kitten's mother. The girl was gone with her box of kittens. With her new kitten in hand, Snow White looked down every aisle for the girl. She even asked the vendors of her whereabouts. No one knew of a young girl with eyes the color of rain and a box of kittens.

The name Vesper Woolf was as natural to the kitten as breathing. She knew her name the moment it popped up in Snow White's head. She also knew all about human moods, needs and faults. She knew her human mother was not in a healthy situation, but wouldn't accept it either.

Vesper was vivacious and spunky. The Demon did whatever he could to "tame" that spunk. He started throwing tantrums over the attention Snow White gave to Vesper. These tantrums were in the same vein as the ones he threw when he thought another man was looking at his Snow White.

Vesper Woolf knew secrets. She knew what happened in that shoddy apartment and she knew what could have happened. Cats are smart, much more so than your average human male. They have the uncanny ability to see the past, eat the present and look into the future. Why else would there be so many superstitions surrounding them? It was a cat that killed the plague-infested rat that clung to St. France's sleeve. It was cats that they burned at the stake with Joan of Arc, and with Witches. When mankind attempted to rid the world of this animal, it was in their absence that the Black Death swept through the Old World. And only a cat can subdue a devil or evil djinn. No wonder Witches keep them as familiars. And that's exactly what young Vesper Woolf intended to do with Demon – send him to his Christian hell.

Demon came to loath the Vesper so much. Snow White glowed when she was around the cat and it irritated him. He went to class when he felt like it, painted occasionally, and mostly hung out in smoky cafes with fellow artists. He had a taste for excessive porn along with anything else vulgar. He was a Christian and could always repent after any sin.

Demon made sure that he kept a tight reign on their domestic life. Any noise that he found annoying was quieted. He picked out all the food that was bought in the house and if he didn't like something of Snow White's he broke it. He would have no "engraved images" in his house. This kept Snow White from decorating with womanish trinkets.

Whenever Snow White thought of something particularly smart or was too happy, he would "correct" her with deriding remarks, a pinch or slap. He had so perfectly broken her down over the last year to mold the living situation he wanted. He had to work for nothing and he shouldn't. His whore mother had mistreated him and pushed him too much. He blamed all women for his neglected childhood. Demon really had not had that bad of a life at all. His childhood was just an exaggerated excuse for him to use people to his advantage.

Demon returned home from spending the evening with his weird friends. He was high on something, but Snow White had never been around drugs and was naïve to the whole subject. He flopped down on the sofa and grabbed the remote from her. After changing the channel he threw it at Vesper who was curled up her basket in the corner of the den. The kitten was too agile for his aim and sprung out of the way.

"Don't do that!" Snow White said sharply. He turned his head slowly to look at her squarely in the face. Demon hit her across the back of the head.

"Shut your damn mouth. You love that cat more than me. I should take that cat for a ride in the car so she can get use to me." His voice changed on the last sentence to a more sinister note. Snow White saw the idea creeping into his head.

"You would have to kill me first." She was dead serious so he let it drop, laughing at her. It made him mad that she'd defy him over mere cat, a womanish animal. He looked over to see her eating a piece of cheese and slapped it from her hand.

"Why are you stuffing your face, fat bitch!" Snow White had never been fat; in fact, she'd always been underweight. But weight is an issue that controls too many women.

"Your legs are so chubby and you're sitting there eating cheese!" He pinched her thigh so hard it left a bruise.

One particular day when Demon picked up Snow White from the bookstore she worked at in her car, she decided she was through, through with him, herself and life in its entirety. Demon had stripped her of every ounce of esteem, worth, and individuality. Either this relationship was over, or her life was over. Demon saw it the same way but with a different spin.

A big fight took place that night. Snow White had held in her despair, rage and suicidal thoughts too long and with their release a thunderstorm broke loose. No one heard the fight or Demon breaking and banging things more than he usually did. He drug Snow White around by her long dark hair and screamed directly into her ears as loud as he could. Vesper Woolf yowled and jumped onto his back - claws ripping - only to be thrown into the wall. Demon was trying to choke Snow White to death. She was as white as death anyway. Snow White had nails almost as sharp as a cat's claws so he gave up and headed to the closest where he stored his bow and arrows. Snow White leaned against the sofa in the den with Vesper above her head. The cat was crouched down in a hunting position.

There was no emotion, no thought, no voice, in Snow White's head at that moment in space and time. Ever since she had become involved with Demon it felt as though she'd been watching her life from afar, like an out of body experience. That wasn't her! It just couldn't be! This was not the same girl that had been the pride and joy of her father, her grandmother's favorite, the Catholic schoolgirl who was praised for her grace. Then she saw that all that had been a lie too. She'd been trained to live her life through the expectations of others. Her mother had never raised her to take abuse from boys and she'd never dreamed of getting married. How had she gotten here and how to you get back? The truth is you never go back to the way it was before.

The rain splattered violently on the dirty windowpanes and the staleness in the apartment air thickened. A shout emerged from the bedroom. Demon had found his hunting bow; the severed string had been gnawed apart by a cat. He flew into the room in a rage. His eyes were bigger than usual, far too big to be human. The pupils were dilated so his eyes looked completely black and the mop of long nappy hair on his head hung in a dark mass. Snow White thought she saw the strands of hair turn into vipers.

Demon picked up the young cat and hurled her into the wall. Snow White cried out in her own rage, the first real emotion she'd felt in over a year. Vesper Woolf bounced back to her feet effortlessly and raised her face to Demon. Even in the darken apartment Snow White could see that the cat's eyes had turned human.

In that moment, Snow White was herself again. The clay cross Demon had made, the only engraved image he would allow in the apartment, turned upside down on the wall and dropped to the floor shattering. Demon, startled by the omen, buckled at the knees and fell to the floor. Snow White watched, holding Vesper from the sofa as lightening struck close outside. It lit up the entire room, and Demon started wailing to whatever had entered with the lightening bolt.

"No, no, no!" He was screaming and frothing at the mouth. "Don't forsake me!!! You can't! I am Who am! I am the chosen!"

The shape shifted to a solid blackness stretching as tall as the ceiling; it's back faced the window, Demon lay on the floor at the feet of the shadow form. Snow White saw the face but no description would be adequate. The voice was low and even, afterward she recalled nothing of what was said. It reached out and gripped Demon's face with a paw of a hand and bent his neck back so sharply that it cracked. Demon shook in spasms and was still shaking when the Being was gone. Snow White gathered her belongings and the kitten with hidden talents she'd named Vesper Woolf. That night was the beginning of the rest of their lives.

A pompous, spoilt and often anal cat looked down on her Mama from the bedroom window of the historical home. The young woman outside was standing on the bricked street under a row of gnarly oaks. She held a four-leaf clover in her hand. It was the third she'd found in the yard since moving into the spacious Victorian. The house behind her was an American gothic style, much like her life story had been. She looked up into the treetops and smiled as another girl moved from the shade of the veranda to stand beside her, wrapping an arm around her waist. The cat smiled a Cheshire grin because for that one moment in time and space on this little plot of dirt, all was right with the world.

THE FOREIGN PRINCE OF ALFHEIM

Morrigan had no intention of taking the mortal child. He was some random colorful trinket that caught her eye through an occasional flight of fancy across The Human Factor. She had circled around twice to observe his brilliant copper head shifting from shades of bronze to gold in the sunlight. His tiny, plump body was too fair to be exposed to such harsh subtropical lighting; the freckles made his pale skin luminous. She glided down on warm air currents, interest growing in the human child. He was in a rough enclosure of some kind, a school yard. Humans made everything ugly and most of their structures contained high levels of iron, much like their frail bodies. She perched on the topmost railing of the fence, watching the small collection of human cubs as she'd watched the hoard of humanity through the ages.

He was plump for his size; shockingly blue eyes bulged out in a pale, round face glistening with sadness from the taunts and threats of the other children. He had surrendered to the shade of an elm, one of the only trees in the dusty school yard. Morrigan noticed that the adults watched the children vacantly without emotion; they were all short and soft females wearing clothing that did nothing for their already unfortunate looks. The Human Factor could always be described as shades of beige no matter what climate zone one ventured into. Excited jeers brought Morrigan's attention back to the fire-headed child. He had a vibrancy to his aura that would fade in time as the mortal world preyed on it. The children – all of them, those with the darkest color skin of umber to the unevenly tanned ones – taunted the ginger one because he was different. His body shook with an instinctive fury at first, a genetic imprint haunting him from the soul of his DNA. His peoples had once been a proud, stolid race who'd known Morrigan all too well. "The Raven Goddess" she'd been to them and her avian form their battle emblem. They had been her pets until they were slaved in the clutches of the soul devouring movements of petty religions. The Sidhe had thought this would prove to be a fast, yet furious phase in human evolution. The mental plague was still with them today, much to the dismay of Others watching the progress, or rather the regression of the upright apes.

Morrigan watched as that instinctive fury faded quickly to fear. And the scent of his fear carried in the wind. Just because they'd forgotten how to consciously smell the emotional reaction of each other didn't mean that they couldn't. The other human offspring closed in like a pack hunters from eons ago from which the upright primates had evolved. She could have just watched or flown away in complete unemotional detachment, but she did not. As the kids advanced, the raven readied herself for flight. She watched as one boy advanced in a leering sneer of slurred taunts; she waited until he began to physically lash out at the descendent of her pets. Then, with a shrill, rapacious battle cry, she dove straight for the face.

The children shrieked in real horror, finally alarming the matronly woman who rushed over to the hoard of little bodies only to duck behind the kids once the dark mass swept down over them. "Vulture!" one began bleating in terror. Morrigan would have grinned if she'd been in her true form. She beat the woman's head again with her wings, enjoying the scent of pure energy streaming in from the mortals beneath her. It had been a long time…and she took her time sucking the emotional upheaval out of the adults and children. When she was bored, she circled back around the elm to perch on a low branch. She wanted to see his reaction. If he paid her any acknowledgment instead of cowering in fear like the others, if so, then he was hers. And he did; the fire-haired boy stared at her in amazement and admiration. She was the biggest "blackbird" he'd ever seen. Bigger than the hawks at the zoo! And she'd saved him.

Morrigan cooed at him softly in her raven form, the large black beak didn't allow for the facial movements; she wanted to reassure him of her fondness of him. She slowly floated to the ground, a couple feet from her chosen pet. The other humans had retreated to the shadowy recesses of the school building, peering out of ashen, fearful faces at the spectacle of the raven and outcast boy. He slowly leaned closer to her, as she advanced agilely, not to frighten him. Then she spoke when she was only inches from him: "Human child, if you follow me now you will never feel sorrow again. I will take care of you and care for you as my own child. Follow me!" Her voice came out of the raven's beak as low and fluid as it would have been if she'd spoken to him in her Sidhe form. She began very slowly to walk to the other side of the tree, which eclipsed the view of the other humans watching from the close distance. The boy, wiping the snot from his nose on his dirty shirt, crawled behind her. The elm was large enough to still hide Morrigan's sleek tallness.

"Listen to me closely," she addressed the child. "I will change shape into a very tall woman. Do not be afraid of me – I have come to save you from a stale fate." The raven watched the child with all black eyes. He was a bit older than what she'd initially thought and she could tell that his mind was processing her words. "Do you understand me?" she asked. The boy nodded slowly and opened his mouth to say something only to shut it again. "It is very important that you make no sound. We do not want to attract the attention of the others, do we?" the raven prepared him. He nodded again, this time sharper. She could hear one of the matrons calling for the boy. The woman was shrill in a frenzy of panic and slowly edging towards the elm.

"Keep your eyes on me." That was the last time she spoke in raven form. Morrigan morphed into her Sidhe form in the blink of an eye. The boy's eyes widen in frozen fear. She swiftly knelt in front of him. "Do not be afraid. I will love you forever." Morrigan opened her long, alabaster arms motioning the boy to embrace her. He began to more towards her and she reached out to him further, taking him into her embrace. They vanished the second the teacher caught a glimpse of the other side of the tree from a safe distance. Her sighting of the Elf picking Ewan up into her elongated arms was such an external aberration of the woman's consciousness and reality that she immediately forgot the sight the moment she saw it. The school officials and witnesses would later report to the grieving parents and community that the boy had disobediently ran away from school grounds on his own accord. There was no prompting by the other children or neglect from the teachers; they argued the child must have been disturbed, which pointed to behavioral problems. Therefore, everyone involved in the bullying and neglect of Ewan could be exonerated of responsibility.

The boy shook in shock for the first few minutes of his absorption into Alfheim. Morrigan slowly sank to the soft, mossy ground. The twilight, lavender blue sky twinkled with stars foreign to a mortal. The twin moons hung adjacent to each other, always together yet never quite touching much like star-crossed lovers. She sang something soft and low, in a strange tongue to Ewan. He gradually became aware of the softness of her long, flimsy dress and skin contrasting the firmness of muscle and bone beneath. The bluish, milk-colored skin of the tall woman sparkled slightly. If he'd had the word in his vocabulary, he would've called it pearlescent. Her black hair was thickly stranded but felt silky as it brushed against his tear-streaked face. She didn't seem to notice the snot that he'd left behind on her bosom.

Ewan slowly looked around, rubbing his eyes in wonderment. There was a rolling landscape that extended out to the high, rocky coastline. The natural floor was thick with low herbal flora and occasionally doted with clusters of enormous trees. They weren't just trees, they were the living home of some denizens of Alfheim. The trunk of one tree could be as big as his parents' entire house. Ewan noticed these healthy giants contained circular houses that tiered upward in landings. These homes looked nothing like his tree house. They were smooth and elegantly designed to blend into the nature surrounding them. Intricate symbols decorated some and charms of seashells and crystals hung in the rounded windows.

His ten year old eyes danced in awe. In the distance, a structure emerged from the rocky coast: a castle hewn out of sea crystals. Morrigan followed his gaze. "Yes, that's where I live," she said softly. He turned to look up at her; she knew he would balk in fear at first. She met his stare as softly as she could, blinking slowing. He gasped at her all black eyes, only the very edges contained whiteness. Her lashes were long and inky thick, like her hair. And her eyebrows looked like the devil's upswept inky brows in the biblical picture book his grandparent's preacher had given him last Christmas. She could read every image he emoted and she pitied his encaged soul full of invented dogmas. Her sharp features were elongated and predatory. To Morrigan, he was a cute but plump little boy who would grow into a broad shouldered and lanky man. In this stage of development, he resembled one of the colorful little goblin children. His bright hair was a mass of loose curls and his brows and lashes were just as red as the hair on his round head. She impulsively snuggled him and was pleased when he did not flinch. It had been a long time since she'd fostered a child and she had missed the surges of maternal fondness she felt for Ewan's kind.

And it was the goblins that Ewan first took up with. Mag's kind took keenly to the young human child. Black Annis, the bogy goblin matron, treated Ewan as one of her own brood when he was in her subterranean domain. She gently chided Morrigan for spoiling the boy, yet doted on him herself. Through his remaining childhood, Ewan's days were spent making mild mischief with the goblin youth, or in the Elven school Morrigan insisted he begin attending once he was well adjusted to Alfheim. He loved her dearly.

Ewan did receive a far superior education than what he would have if he'd remained with his own kind. As a young man, he excelled at sciences as well as swordplay. His goblin friend, Grim, lamented when Ewan surpassed his own short height. As Morrigan had predicted, Ewan grew to be a tall and quite handsome young lad, and even at eighteen the elf ladies all had their eyes on him. He was beginning to return their glances as well. Morrigan was not pleased with this and made it known in her kingdom that her fosterling was indeed to be reserved for herself. The Dark Elves, who she reigned over, complied. However, the occasionally sylph or dryad would silkily emerge into Ewan's space whenever he frequented the environs of Alfheim. And in the neighboring crystalline cities, the elf maidens' curiosity drew them to the only human currently in Alfheim – and not just any human, but the fostering prince of The Morrigan, The Dark Queen.

And so, it was the latter predicament with one of the elf maidens of white locks, that Ewan became briefly enthralled with. Her name was Ninevah and she encouraged his affections. She was long and sleek like all the elves, her eyes a searing yellow. She pinned her long white hair up on her head, allowing it to trickle down her supple spine. Ewan did not find her as elegant as his foster mother, but there was an attraction between them that ignited his physical appetite for the first time. Ninevah would only meet him deep in the forest, underneath a water fall. And there she would mirthlessly tease him, allowing him to touch her there and kiss her here, but never returned his affections.

Grim would patiently stand guard, lest Ninevah's consort discover her infidelities with the human. And one day the elf's consort did follow his mate. Leveling the short and stocky goblin to the ground with one blow, the elf followed his lover underneath the waterfall only to discover Ewan's lips on her milky throat and his hand venturing under her flimsy garments. The enraged elf roared out in rage, exposing all his pointed teeth as Ninevah stumbled out excuses. Ewan froze. The elf man was horrific, and suddenly he remembered the lore of his distant human past. He stumbled to stand as the elf advanced; his six fingered hands were wrapped around Ewan's weaker human neck before he could attempt to sprint. Suddenly, there was Grim, his short, green body hobbling before the dark figure treading lightly behind him.

There she was, The Morrigan. "Stop." She commanded and the elf obeyed, slowly yet surely releasing Ewan. He turned, still seething. He managed a curt nod of the head at The Dark Queen standing before him. The slick wetness of the rocks did not impede her stance. She was in front of the trembling Ninevah, and within a flash, backhanded the elf maid. The words Morrigan spoke to the elf in High Elven were as offending as Ninevah's seduction of her fostering. The she-elf forgotten after her reprimanding, Morrigan turned to the elf man. "This human is mine. If you make discord with him, then you do so with me. "

Morrigan was a fantastically, horrifyingly beautiful sight when mad, as Ewan had seen her at her court only a couple times. Something about her rage excited him and he found his body reacting in new ways that confused him.

"He should be punished." The man elf growled; his orange eyes bright slits and his sharp features took on a serpentine quality.

"He will be. But that is my concern." Morrigan's attire was dark; her long tunic over tight riding pants and high boots equipped her for a brawl. "You do not want quarrel with me. I can destroy your bloodline." The elf queen smiled at the implications she made.

The male elf replied only with a quick bow. He exited the cave. Morrigan turned back to Ewan. "Come," she said sternly. Neither paid the whimpering Ninevah notice. Once outside the waterfall, Morrigan left Ewan to stumble down the slippery bank by himself. Grim had hid himself in the nearest hallow tree; he'd shared the old stories of Morrigan with Ewan before, rumors she would not speak of regarding her past involvement with humanity. Ewan watched from the creek's wide bank as Morrigan shifted into her raven form and was gone in the blink of an eye.

Grim snorted as he stuck his head out. His large eyes were comical with fear, except Ewan could not find it in himself to laugh. "You are in much troubles!" Grim gasped, peering anxiously at the sky.

Ewan only replied, "I have to go." And he ran all the way to Morrigan's crystal palace. He stopped when he reached the courtyard, debating on which door to take. He knew the intricate maze of the palace intimately. Would she be in her study that was located in the highest turret? He chose the twisting back staircases leading into one of the higher halls. The palace was sparsely furnished and vegetation grew freely in the unused rooms. He deftly entered the floor Morrigan made her main home. The lighting was recessed and dim; artwork from all ages of humanity adorned the walls. He knew which room was her very private chamber: a large one tucked any at the end of the hall. The door was ajar, but he knocked anyway.

He knew she was allowing him to hear her movement by the stone fireplace, shadows of her form danced on the wall opposite of her. Ewan noted that she turned her head slightly from the movement of her lithe shadow. He suddenly realized that he was holding his breath. She had never had to firmly chastise him before and knowing her temper, he was for the first time fearful that she would.

"Come in, Ewan," she said softly and low.

He did as she bid. Ducking his head sheepishly, he began to ramble an apology. "I'm so sorry. I just...I was...."

"You don't have to apologize for having desires. Perhaps it is my fault; I have not taught you the ways of the flesh. I was waiting till you were ready, apparently you are." Morrigan looked at him lovingly. He did adore her.

She motioned for him to approach her, he did. She hugged him, running her long fingers through his long copper curls. He had grown into a young man, as tall as she and well muscled. He consciously realized that she no longer was taller than he nor did she seem older. Morrigan was ageless. She hadn't changed since the day she'd saved him from the mob in the schoolyard making him a prince. He lowered his head to rest it on her shoulder. She'd always smelled like verbena and frankincense. Her hands lowered to her neck and shoulders gently caressing him and then to his hardened biceps. He noticed for the first time that she'd changed from her previous attire into a typical light slip of a dress that lady elves seemed to prefer. The top was thin and a bit snug as the bottom flowed loosely around her legs and feet. Ewan felt that odd sensation again growing inside of him.

Morrigan knew the change in his perception of her before he did. Moving her hands up and down his arms, she gazed levelly into his blue eyes. "Are you hungry?"

Ewan smiled. "For you," he replied instinctively, then only to blush at his boldness.

Morrigan's eyes twinkled with amusement. "You have more of an education than what I thought."

Ewan looked down. "Well, I do hang out with the goblins and they talk about such things."

Morrigan sniffed. "The goblins have a rather unrefined notion of such things."

Ewan actually took the raven goddess by surprise with his response. "Then why don't you teach me the refined version."

She smiled slowly and began to peel off his shirt, caressing his chest and waist. Their lips met at the same time and she wove her fingers through his hair as he kissed her. He was a natural at the art; that cannot be said for many men. She let his hands explore her curves as she unfastened his pants. After she had shown him pleasures that made him completely malleable in her hands, he stumbled to take off her slip as she gradually led him to the canopied bed.

He parted her sleek legs and entered her in a frenzy of physical sensations he'd new felt before.

She wrapped her legs around him tightly, writhing in response to his thrusts. And his mouth found hers again and then her breasts. She held him fast in her arms as he hardened again. They danced beneath the sheets until the first pink of dawn peeked over the horizon of sea.

Morrigan's long, ink hair was plastered across the pillows. Her eyes cat slits as she rested in that lucid sleep that elves do. Ewan had fallen asleep on her flat abdomen, his hand in between her warm thighs. He felt the urge again, struggling atop her again, he whispered in a pointed ear: "I love you." Morrigan smiled with her full lips in her lucid state. "You do," she replied in his mind. "But you also loved this." And she pulled him down into her again.

He had everything he could ever want and a fairy kingdom to go with it. But it is only natural that a young man such as Ewan should grow restless with his entire human life before him. However, in Alfheim he did not age to an elderly fate. He began to think of his human family and the world that he left behind. Morrigan had given him a kingdom and for that he should be happy. And he was happy, though incomplete. The restlessness of his humanity was overcoming Ewan and The Dark Queen saw this.

She alighted next to him on the pearly shore, as he starred in the twinkling sky of Alfheim for the last time. "I may regret this," Ewan began.

"Sometimes you have to lose what you love in order to appreciate your love," Morrigan offered quietly. "If you don't go, you will always think about leaving. I have given you the life that the poets of your world dream of... but you, young Ewan, are the kind of man who must make his own way. And I will always be close by."

He turned to look into her black eyes. "I don't want to forget you." Taking her face in his hands, Ewan's blue eyes glazed with tears. "Will I remember all of this?"

"Oh yes. You will remember. But it will be like a dream." Morrigan brushed her lips against his, bringing him into her lithe embrace. "And when you are finished, you will return home to the Summer Country. I do fear once you are there you will always ache for here."

Ewan shivered with the thought of what he was giving up by going to the world of man again. "I cannot hide here. I feel like that is what I am doing."

"I know," Morrigan breathed. "When it is time, I will come and bring you back home."

With that, Morrigan pulled him from her. "Walk into the sea." Ewan had swam in the waters surrounding the keep his entire childhood. But this time was different. Morrigan parted the foam crested waves for Ewan's footfalls as his human senses saw the tunnel in the near distance. The other side was invisible and as he approached the opening, Ewan paused, looking back to Morrigan but the sea had closed and a ringing began, a ringing that roared his consciousness into the depth of the tunnel until he was stumbling, then falling as the ringing grew to a terrifying crescendo....

He threw the alarm clock into the wall where it dented the cheap apartment drywall and shattered. The bed linens were a tangled mess of sweat and old semen stains. Sally had stayed last night – again. And Tara the night before that, however, neither supposedly knew of the other. He preferred to keep it that way. And there was Sally now, standing half nude in the doorway of his bedroom. Her lips poised for the questions, a dash of fear in her eyes.

"What?" He groaned.

"That was a bit excessive," Sally chastised. She glanced at the broken clock; Ewan glared at it.

He propped himself, his taut freckled arm decorated with a sleeve of tattoos, his personal favorite being a coiled serpent that winded down his forearm. He ran his hand through his loose red curls. He kept his hair on the long side. It pissed off old people and got him laid, two good things. Ewan shrugged, "Did you make coffee?" He asked as though he had not just chucked his alarm clock into the wall.

"Don't change the subject." Sally was adamant. "It was another one of those dreams, right? The one with the beautiful woman?" Sally's hazel eyes glistened whenever he spoke of that other world whereas Tara's grew cold with jealousy.

"Yeah," he admitted. "I did. I was speaking with her again. No sex this time."

Sally sighed. "You really should write this dream place down. You are very lucky, Ewan. Not so many people are blessed with such a gift." She moved to him; her thighs were almost as pale as his.

The flannel shirt she donned was open. His hand moved to caress one of her inner thighs.

"You believed in unicorns as a little girl, didn't you?" Ewan teased her. Sally smiled. "I still do." Her eyes were glistening again, but for another reason. Ewan smiled crookedly as he worked his hand upward.

"Well, we don't have to worry about time anymore," Ewan teased, pulling Sally on top of him. She shook off his shirt, grabbing his shoulders. Her thighs were now wrapped around his sides and as she moved across his pelvis, his hand clutching her waist. "Time is ours right now."

Tara eyed the apartment critically again. "You really should do something about the décor, or lack of." As typical pop culture, wanna-be princess, she'd been trying her hand at the Indie look and it wasn't working out well for her. The leggings and boho dress would have suited Sally, but Tara just looked silly.

"And you should stick to your slut look. It actually compliments you," Ewan smirked. Tara glared at him, folding her arms across her chest. They had an extremely toxic relationship that benefited neither party.

"You are so unworthy of me. How dare you..." Tara started, her eyes slits.

"Yet you continue to come back for more." Ewan smiled widely, lounging on his second-hand sofa, arms propped behind his head.

"I don't love you," she uttered.

"That's okay. There are plenty of women that do," Ewan replied nonchalantly. "I never count on a woman loving me, just fucking me."

With that, Tara slung her purse over her shoulder, hoisting her book bag on the other. "I'm so not missing class for this. Have fun with that dense little twit Sally."

"I will!" Ewan called after her as she slammed the door. He knew that Tara was running down the dirty carpeted stairwell and onto the crooked cement steps. By now she was half-trotting to her car in a parking lot full of shabby vehicles. She'd turn on the air conditioner and sit in her car sobbing for a good ten minutes hoping Ewan would fly down the steps after her and apologize, taking her into his arms and confessing that she was his only love.

Ewan enjoyed the view of the hot pavement jungle from his set of open windows. They both knew that she did this with every guy, compensating for something that she lacked inside. Sometimes he was convinced it was a heart. Girls like Tara were too shallow to truly love anything other the couture consumerism. Temporarily, his thoughts drifted to Sally and her chestnut waves, but they always landed on the ethereal woman in his dreams. He'd looked for her in so many women, older ones and younger ones alike. Maybe he should just be happy with Sally. She was genuine and kind, not trendy and fake like so many others. But then he would grow tired of her, and he'd hurt her in the end like he had so many times before.

Ewan glanced at his watch; she was in class now anyway. It is better to let Sally have a life. He breathed through the window screen. "Find someone who deserves you, Sal. It's not me."

Ewan awoke after another dream. The images were foggy; he could only recall a ghostly coastline and twilight sky behind it. He groaned as he rolled over. Another head of head greeted him. It was only Olivia. He slapped his hand down on his forehead. Why did he do this to himself? She was another needy but good girl. Tara may deserve to be treated like a tramp, but Olivia did not. She stirred beside him, "Why are you awake?"

Ewan sighed. "Why are you awake to notice I'm awake?" He didn't feel like having a conversation with her.

Olivia pouted. "Sorry."

Ewan groaned again and tucked his arm around her. "It's okay." He then realized the one reason that he liked for girls to spend the night. After a couple minutes of snuggling, they were having sex again. The next morning Ewan would make excuses as to why he did not want a relationship.

Ten years passed in a blink. Ewan was older and still single. He could never quite cure the restlessness that stirred in his chest for another place, another time. He knew that he'd failed both his parents' expectations, ending up as a tattoo artist in Ashville. And there were still the women...occasionally he thought of Sally, wondering what happened to her. She was the only one he thought deeply about, other than the fairy woman of his dreams. He remembered the last time they'd fucked. And for some reason, that made him ashamed. Ewan hoped that Sally had grown up to find a man who deserved her. Most of his friends had families, were starting families, or getting divorces now. At least Ewan didn't have to deal with the former.

There were still women; whiney ones who wanted to settle down, and wild ones that just wanted a good time. He kept the company of both. But he couldn't find her in any of them. The woman who invaded his dreams evaded his reality. He had a few successful art shows in several major cities and one collection of poetry published.

It wasn't for twenty more years until she came for him, compassion in her all-black eyes. Ewan was a washed up, old man of regrets. He'd formed no meaningful bonds, using women and competing with men. In his dank, city apartment, she found him. The Morrigan was regal and ageless in her pristine white gown. Ewan's head was slack from the bottle of whisky he'd feasted on that day. He'd long lost the firmness of youth to alcohol and drugs. The sun had blasted his fair skin to leathery wrinkles. Ewan had played hard, too hard.

"And now you are ready to return to our kingdom?" Her voice was smooth and deep.

Ewan was too familiar with its sultry tones; this was the voice that had haunted his dreams. Once, a girl named Sally had wanted to hear it too. "I was ready over a decade ago. Why come to me like this?"

"Because you had to live, Ewan, you wanted to live your mortal life. If you've misused it in any way, those were your decisions. There is no time or place for regrets. You will only linger as a discarnate if you allow ill emotions to overcome you." The Morrigan approached, running gentle fingers through his white, thin hair. "Come home. It is time."

"I don't deserve it...no more beauty. I craved this world and used up all beauty I found here. I've hurt too many." Ewan moaned as tears spilled down his face.

"So now you want me to be your godhead, your judge and jury?" Morrigan spoke with firmness. "I do not toy in such ways with you poor creatures. And I will right your wrongs because I love you, all of you."

The room was growing intensely dark now. There was only one point of light, and She was standing in it. "Come home, Ewan."

Like a serpent, he shed his skin. Ewan walked into the light holding Morrigan's long hand. And then he was the young man before his fall, all tall, fair, and lean. The twin moons shown brightly over the sea in a lavender sky; in the distance Sally waved to him. He was home.

CINDERELLA IN HELL

There have been and are many Cinderellas, each in her own hell, and there will be more to come. There is something delicious in the combination of extreme beauty and innocently good that attracts real world vampires and demons (a.k.a. seething jealous people), who desire no less to torment, control, possess, or completely destroy Beauty because they cannot have it. They are not it and this drives them mad.

Our Cinderella lives a nondescript life but she attracts the weird to her as most charismatic people do. Cinderellas come in various colors. Some are curvaceous babes with natural honey hair, others are olive complexioned with dark eyes that tilt like a cat's, but our Cinderella has hair the color of a maple leaf in autumn, skin as white as a lily and eyes the color of the first spring rain. She's as lithe as an alley cat, tall like a reed and her face would fair well on the front a fashion magazine. Rella is too good to be true, and good meaning inside and out; she is as pure on the inside as her lily complexion is on the outside.

Rella is loathed by women, who because of her innocent nature, doesn't usually catch their candy-coated insults and when she does, thinks it must be her fault. She doesn't know that there is such a culture of women because it is not in her nature to act accordingly. The envious women turn around her naiveté and defame Rella by hailing her as stupid and slow. "She is beautiful so therefore she must be dumb." They nod in agreement amongst themselves and to their men.

Men would like to eat her. Rella is, by men, reflected into many personas like a prism catching rays of light. To the predators she is the ultimate prey. They see the white aura surrounding her and her otherworldly beauty. She is the White Buffalo. If only they can catch her and spoil her. Some would keep her, locking and knocking her up. Others, when finished with her, would toss her back into the wind leaving her with nothing.

Rella would have very few friends over the course of her life. Her story is not about her lack of friends so much as it is about her enemies.

1995

Rella, a senior in high school, was for the first time tasting some of the bittersweet freedoms that come with being an adult. She was seventeen and in the twilight of her school days. From her current vantage point, there was so much brilliance in life. The unknown, the un-experienced, shown like a beacon in flashes throughout her thoughts.

"I need to live." She muttered to herself, looking onto the rainy sky from the cafeteria window.

Across from her, Duncan looked up from his taco. "What?"

Blinking, Rella turned to him. "Oh, nothing. I was just talking to myself."

Shrugging, he returned to his taco and listening to Kyle's critique of the upcoming season finale of *Babylon 5*. "I think that G'Kar is the character who will completely morph, even more so than Delenn. Just wait, by the end of the series he'll be all together a different person," Kyle predicted, wagging a finger at Duncan who just snorted.

"Whatever, I just prefer the original commander."

"Oh, look, Teri, the geeks are talking politics!" The pack of "pretty" girls with bleached hair passed Rella's table. They spoke of the guys seated with her but looked at Rella. Their eyes always sought her out, studying her wishfully thinking if they studied Rella long enough their eye sockets might just suck her beauty into them. As for Rella, she hardly noticed them anymore. When the popular girls noticed no one was paying them the attention they deemed themselves worthy of, they walked on whispering among themselves with occasional glances back to the table of geeks and Rella.

"You okay, Eel?" She looked up at Kyle's use of her nickname. They gave everyone who was in the geek group nick-names.

"Yeah, just pensive." She sighed, cupping her chin in her palm. "Don't you ever get impatient with things? I wish sometimes I could be out of college tomorrow and I haven't even started."

Duncan looked up at her from his lunch tray. Self-consciously he wiped his chin and nose with a wadded up napkin. "I think I know what you mean. It's like you just want life to hurry up and get over with."

"No, not quite. It's more than that. I wanted to really experience freedom. You know, complete independence with no one breathing down my neck." Rella's brow knitted in thought, "That's the only way I can describe want I'm feeling."

"My dad says no one is ever really free. There's always something: taxes, people dressed up like Jesus on street corners yelling at you, mother-in-laws, bad bosses going through menopause...did I say taxes?" Kyle pushed his glassed back up to the top of his nose. "Sorry, I don't mean to take a dump on your angst-filled day-dreams."

"No, I've heard all that before. I just can't believe that it is true. Not yet, anyway." Rella smiled weakly. Kyle mirrored her smile, noticing how her eyes twinkled in the light from the window. She had the attention of the other guys at the table now. Kyle recalled that she always did when she spoke. The only thing they had ever held against her was the fact she that considered the premise of *Deep Space 9* superior to that of *The Next Generation.*

"We'll all soon find out anyway. Only two more months...we're at childhood's end." Duncan observed.

James spoke up from the end of the table a few thoughts behind the rest. "Hey, what is menopause anyway?"

1997

Her childhood was a lifetime ago. Sometimes through the haze that was her life, she caught glimpses of it. If she were to step back in time, she would not recognize herself. Rella still looked the same but the look behind her eyes had changed. It had become deeper.

"I'm not paying you to stand there and look pretty!" The older woman snapped.

"I'm just cleaning off the counter," Rella replied hurriedly as she picked up the spray bottle and rag.

"I don't care what you're doing, I told you to put together those new displays." Glenda was a foot shorter but she seemed to be looming over Rella.

"I was...I mean I am. Betty just had to use the restroom and called me up here to watch her register for her," Rella stammered. Glenda's only reply was a pig-like snort. She had after all instructed her employees to always call for replacements during breaks. Betty returned just in time and Rella, realizing that she had been holding her breath, exhaled. Betty, being a senior citizen, moved slowly. Glenda was tapping her boot loudly. "Betty, I'd appreciate it if you would report to me when you need a restroom break." Glenda spoke louder than what she needed to.

"I'm old but I ain't deaf yet," Betty said winking at Rella, patting the girl's arm companionably.

Glenda turned to Rella. "You can get back to work now." She was still glaring.

Rella did just that. The two displays were in the back of the store by the magazines. She was working on both a mystery and a science fiction one. The shelves were tricky being made of a cheap plastic, but it didn't take her long to arrange them.

"Girl, what you doin'?" Rella turned. Yolanda grinned, hands in her uniform apron.

Rella couldn't help but return her grin noticing Yolanda's gold tooth. "Just working on my displays," Rella replied.

"Heard the Bitch got to you? Betty was talkin' bout it. I would've told that wide-load to kiss my entire ass!" Yolanda slapped her own ample hiney in emphasis. Rella giggled. Only Yolanda could get away with such blatant protests.

"What are you doing?" she asked placing books on the last shelf.

"Absolutely, nothing till my shipment gets here. I'll have too much to do then so I ain't goin' be wearing myself out," Yolanda replied loudly twirling one her braids through her fingertips. "Girl, you so skinny. How you do it?" Yolanda asked, talking to Rella while finished her displays.

Rella blushed. "I don't know...genetics probably." She said, pausing self-consciously to tighten her long ponytail.

"Here comes someone." Yolanda grimaced, moving to the other side of the aisle to avoid whoever it may be. Rella turned back to her empty boxes and began to break them down when she felt a hard tap on her shoulder. Rella turned to face a middle-age woman, peering at her. "Where is this book?" She thrust a piece of paper at Rella, who took it. "I think we may be out of this title, but let me check in the back to make sure," Rella replied handing the paper back to the woman.

"I didn't ask you if it was out of stock, I asked you where it is." The woman flicked her shortly cropped hair. You could see her dark roots.

Rella blinked confused. "This would be in fiction if it's in stock. We've had it on a special display since Oprah's featuring of it and have sold out twice. I'll find one for you though."

"Then do so," the woman said shrilly, hands on her hips.

Rella passed the shelf Yolanda was standing behind, "It's in the back, last night's shipment," she whispered to Rella.

Rella found a copy in a box just opened. "Those are not yours." Glenda was behind her as fast as a water snake gliding across water. "I know. I just was getting one for a customer. They're out up front again," she explained weakly.

Glenda nodded slowly as if she was checking Rella's words for hidden meanings. Her gaze moved up and down the girl's figure. She was standing there wide-eyed in front of her like a doe caught in headlights. The beautiful are always stupid, Glenda thought to herself. "Okay, Rella, you just make sure that you tell Yolanda to mark this one off the inventory or you'll mess up our records." Rella nodded and hurried off through the double doors. Glenda shook her head, watching her scurry off. "Stupid girl," the middle-management goddess muttered.

Rella trotted back to the customer who was still waiting by her displays. The woman's glare never left her as she approached. "I thought you had forgotten me."

"No ma'am, I just had to find it." Rella handed her the book but the woman was not done with her yet.

"Why are these not on display? You're working on this...stuff and not restocking these?" The woman questioned, motioning to the science fiction books with a scowl on her face. It made her look like a wrinkled prune.

"I was just assigned this genre. We have a new shipment in of your book... we just received it. They're unpacking boxes in the back." Rella spoke cautiously, scared that the woman would complain to her more.

The woman huffed, shaking her head. "Oprah reported that all bookstores should have this on a special display. I think I need to speak with your manager." The woman narrowed her eyes at Rella.

"You want to meet Glenda?" Rella balked. She couldn't believe the woman was making such a big deal over the availability of this book when she had one.

"If that's your superior, then yes, I want to meet her!" the woman snapped at her.

"Okay, I'll be right back with her," Rella promised numbly. She rushed to the back again. Yolanda was at the pile of boxes across the storage room from her. "Hey, where is Glenda?" Yolanda was unusually quiet. She looked past Rella, motioning with her eyes. Glenda was already halfway to her when she turned around.

"Glenda, there's a customer who would like to inquire about the availability of a book," Rella said, wiping the beads of perspiration off her brow. She heard Yolanda cough stiffly behind her.

Glenda rolled her eyes. "Would this be the same customer you were helping a minute ago?"

"Yes," Rella answered.

"She has her book. What's the problem now?" Glenda was standing arms akimbo with a scowl on her face.

Rella gulped loudly. "She says Oprah says we should always have the books on display up front." Yolanda coughed again and Glenda's scowled deepened. Rella thought that she resembled a bulldog.

"Where is she?" Glenda growled.

"By my displays." Rella felt dizzy.

"Lead the way." Glenda motioned to Rella with her arm.

Rella closed her eyes tightly. She still didn't feel like she was at home. She pulled the sheets tighter over her head to block out the noise and lights from the den. Dave was watching television of course. He sat there everyday in his usual spot.

Glenda had informed her that she would have to redo her displays over tomorrow. The older woman had told her that they looked "stupid." Rella was beginning to hate everybody. They all were out to get her. No matter how much she smiled, how nice she was, they all reacted like rabid dogs. The most hurtful aspect was that Rella was honestly being the best person she could be and it was killing her.

She stopped the tears, as Dave's footfalls closed in on her. He stopped by her head. "Hey, why you hiding?" he demanded.

"I just have a headache. I've had a hard day." She breathed.

"Yeah, I know I had to hear you bitch about it when you got home," Dave retorted. "You shouldn't try to dump all your problems on me. I don't need them. You know how hard I'm looking for a job."

Rella stuck her head out. "You must be looking real hard using the television as your number one resource. Too bad you can't get a letter of recommendation from Springer."

Dave exploded. He lowered his head right beside her ear and yelled, "Don't you disrespect me, you bitch! You always come home tired, saying you've been on your feet all day at work! I don't fuckin' care! You're probably flirting with every dick that walks in that store!" Rella jumped back to the other side of the bed. He reached to grab her but missed. "Fuck you, whore. All you have is your looks and their going." He stormed out of the room, kicking the wall before exiting. Rella felt as if she were in the eye of a tornado.

1998

She wasn't really in the eye of the tornado until the day she kicked Dave out of her life. She didn't have much, especially after he stole most of her belongings, but she lived in a cheap studio apartment on the bad side of town with two cats that adopted her. Rella was not happy, but she was content. Gwen, the blue haired lesbian, was sitting at her one table drinking day old coffee out of a chipped mug.

"So, you got how many more years of school?" asked Gwen.

Rella sighed, looking up from her needlepoint. "At least three if I'm lucky. Dave messed me up with all that. I have to retake a couple classes. However, I'm considering trade school." Rella mused the last sentence aloud.

"That's smart. I know too many college grads with bachelors that ain't getting jack from the workforce." Gwen slurped the cold coffee.

Rella looked up at her. "I don't see how you drink that."

Gwen grinned. "It's easy. Just put it to your mouth, open lips and pour it in."

Rella laughed. "Very funny, smart-ass. I told you to make a fresh pot."

"And let day old coffee go to a waste!" Gwen gasped in mock horror.

Rella shook her head. "My life is a mad dance. At least all has been quiet on the home-front since I've moved and severed some ties."

"Your life will always have some Twin Peakish flavor to it. It's like you invoke something in people without meaning to. You're unaware of the effect you have on people, Rella. Especially straight people. Women hate you and men want to pervert you." Gwen shook her head. "Look at you sitting there sewing like you're out of time. Rella, you really are The Innocent. Life always shits on you and you don't get it."

"I'm beginning to think it isn't life, it is the people, Gwen. I don't seem to find a lot of good these days. I don't get it. It's not like I hang out at bars or ask for uncomfortable situations, they just always find me." Rella's eyes moistened.

This made Gwen uncomfortable. She wanted to go over and hug her, but afraid it would make Rella uncomfortable as well. So, instead she offered an explanation. "And it is always those with the best of intentions, the ones that mean nothing but good that people love to rip into." Gwen winced, realizing she wasn't helping. "I'm sorry. Look, you've got a new life, a new job. Don't dwell on what happened last year."

Rella tried to take Gwen's advice. Her new job was of an independent contractor nature. She cleaned the houses of pampered housewives. Rella became highly recommended among them. One particular client would give her clothes once she tired of them. Her name was Sandy, and she constantly talked in her Yankee accent, following Rella from room to room, as she cleaned. Sometimes the subject was her bastard husband and sometimes it involved her sister's drinking problem.

"She's taking valium again! Any doctor should know not to give that woman valium," Sandy sighed wringing her hands. "I just know she's going to overdose one of these nights."

Then Sandy would move on to another topic all together. "How I would love to fix you up with my son if only he weren't with that slut." At least this was the topic today. Sandy sat sipping on her chai tea as Rella cleaned the sink. She could feel Sandy's eyes on her back. "Rella, let me ask you a question. Please understand that I do not intend any insult by this - but what why are you living like this?" Rella looked over her shoulder at Sandy.

"What do you mean?" Rella blinked.

Sandy looked a bit embarrassed. "I mean, what is a young beauty like yourself doing cleaning houses for a living?" Hurriedly she added, "I know that you're a student and all, but why this?"

Rella straightened. "Because it beats working for someone else. When I worked retail people were so cruel for no reason."

Sandy nodded as if she understood. "Just know you deserve better. I know you don't come from much but that doesn't mean with your talents you can't move up. I have some friends I could fix you up with. What do you say?"

"Well, I don't know if I'm ready to be involved with a guy again. They're so mean. I don't understand why women fight over them." Rella turned back to the sink.

Sandy smiled gently at the girl's back. "Rella, you are a real work of art." Just then the bell rang. "Excuse me a minute."

Rella could hear Sandy talking to one of her tennis friends from the hallway. They were headed to the kitchen. "Rella, this is a very good friend of mine, Mrs. Kimberly Dunlap."

Rella turned around to offer her best smile. "I'd shake your hand, but I've got Clorox all over mine. Nice to meet you."

"Kimberly, take it from me, this is the best little maid you could ask for. She's more reliable than those cleaning services," Sandy recommended beaming at Rella.

"And I'm always available within a day's notice," Rella added.

Kimberly offered Rella a half smile. Turning to Sandy she asked, "Did you get your hair trimmed?"

"Yes, the other day."

"Well, it doesn't even look like it. Where did you go? I don't intend to patron that place." Kimberly inquired rhetorically, her gaze shifting across the elegant kitchen and landing on Rella narrowly.

Rella started to feel uneasy. "Would you like some coffee or tea, like Sandy?" she offered.

"Oh, Rella, you don't have to serve us." Sandy smiled motioning Kimberly to a seat at the oak table.

"Well, you said she was a maid, Sandy." Kimberly sounded a bit peeved. She flicked a lock of highlighted hair out of her face and turned back to Rella. "I'll have coffee." With that, she dismissed the younger woman from her attention.

Making coffee gave Rella an opportunity to see what women like Sandy and Kimberly have to talk about. She noticed it was all mainly gossip about the other wives of the golf club where their husbands both belonged. Both were similar in build, not fat but not slender either, tan, lots of jewelry and urbanite clothing. They wore the kind of causal dress attire you'd see in a fashion magazine. Sandy was different though, a dark brunette she seemed more seasoned and real. Kimberly was trying hard to look younger than she was. Rella knew that were both around forty-five. That wasn't old at all! She didn't understand why they worried so about their age.

"Would you like a cup too, Sandy?" Rella asked.

"Yes, dear. I tell you, Kim, she's the best."

Kimberly snorted looking at Rella, "Honey, I'd never hire a maid that looked like you."

2000

I am coming out of the eye of the storm, Rella thought to herself. She was still a student studying English. She felt like her wheels were going to stop spinning right into a brick wall. This year, she had dated two guys. One spread nasty lies about her among all their mutual friends and then had given her phone number out to his friends. Rella had to get an unlisted number. The other turned out to be a mama's boy.

Rella was at peace with the possibility of being alone. After all, she had learned the hard way that being alone was preferable to being in a bad relationship. She was musing over this while walking to her women's studies class in Holt Hall. Rella had to take a couple of electives for her degree and thought that she might find some female friends in such a class that had similar lives and experiences. Rella was too much of a Pollyanna to think that many of students taking such a course would not turn out to be embittered, jealous women who were looking to blame their unhappiness on something other than their own lack of responsibility.

Rella sat in the corner front of the class beside the window. She was the first one there this particular morning and took advantage of the quiet time to study. The room began to gradually fill up with students. The class consisted of rough looking women, hippies and one gay guy. Rella had spoken with several of the other various students, thinking that she had similarities in common with them but they did not seem interested in wanting to befriend her. In fact, she felt a wave of outright enmity from most of them.

The professor finally arrived a few minutes late as usual with her disheveled stack of papers along with a disheveled head of hair. She was tall and very stocky with a perpetual scowl on her face accept for when she was laughing at one of her own jokes. Hastily she took role then giving the class a thin smile, "Today we're examining gender roles." Rella heard the big girl behind her stand to crank open the old window. The building was old and musty.

"Need some help?" she asked after hearing the girl grunt. The only response Rella got was a glare so she turned back around.

"Let's begin by going counter clockwise around the room and each give a little synopsis of our essays regarding gender and our own unique life experiences." The professor's eyes fell on the gay guy, Bailey, at the other end of the front role.

"I prepared some notes for today," he said in an airy voice, standing.

The professor beamed. "Wonderful."

Bailey stood and gave a wordy account of his childhood and how he was bullied because he was "girlie." Then he recounted how he figured out he was gay, because he always had crushes on guys. Bailey's account ended with him shedding a few tears along with some of the other students. The scene strangely reminded Rella of a protestant fundamentalist witnessing in front of a congregation. She thought of how different he was from her dear Gwen who had suffered much the same plight. Gwen didn't like to talk about her sexual orientation though.

There were four other students to present in front of Rella. She hoped that they would be as wordy as Bailey, taking up the rest of the hour. One student recounted how she had always felt like she was suppose to measure up to some impossible goal because she read fashion magazines as an adolescent and her parents had emotionally scarred her. Two others told of similar experiences. Rella glanced up at the clock, as the hippie in front of her gave a rundown on her essay. Rella looked down at her own paper in her hands. She had not known what to write regarding gender and her experiences. Sure, it was a factor but so were a lot of other issues as well. The hippie finished sooner than the others had, leaving plenty of time for Rella.

Rella cleared her voice, but stayed seated. "Well...um...my essay was about some of the theories we discussed in class and just my experiences as a young adult." She looked expectantly at the professor, smiling weakly.

Dr. Fowler cocked her head at Rella. "What theories did you use?"

"Um...the nature vs. nurturer and engendered social roles. A lot of what we've studied...made me question some things. You know, like growing up Catholic and the way people interact," Rella finished, thinking she was through but Dr. Fowler wasn't finished with her.

"What specifically did you say in your essay regarding your own experience with being typecast by gender, or do you feel like you haven't been that bothered by the gender rules that engulf our society?" Fowler's voice was tighter than usual and her eyes would not leave any part of Rella's seated body alone. A couple girls wearing baggy clothes snickered from the back of the room.

"Well, I wrote a bit about high-school and then just my experiences since," Rella replied neutrally.

"Rella, I'm asking for an opinion, a stand from you, not some wish-washy bantering." Fowler sighed, shaking her head.

"Oh, I included some of that is my essay." Rella was eager to rectify any misunderstanding she may have given the professor of her essay. "I explain in here how people in general just have hang-ups regarding anyone who is different from them. How the particular hang-up depends on the group that you're around. You know, like how people regard you depends on their opinion of themselves as much as it does their feelings toward you."

"No, we don't know. Please elaborate for us." Fowler smiled showing her teeth. Her voice was pleasant but taut. Rella didn't like how she used third person to include the rest of the class.

"Well, I think both genders, or sexes, have seemed negative to me at certain times during my life. Sometimes women are worse to other women than men can be and…"

She was interrupted by Fowler, "How would it sound if you said 'all black people are this way or that'!" The statement was a rhetorical question that Rella had no clue how to answer.

"Huh?" Rella blinked.

Fowler smirked, thinking that beauty could never be accompanied by brains. She simply stood at the podium and glared at the young woman who deserved to be humiliated because she was a living, breathing model that made other women feel inferior. She was going to stare at Rella until the girl said something else just as stupid that she could rip into.

Rella gulped, "All I meant was women bully other women like men do."

"Watch it! You're about to be asked leave the room." The professor smirked and the other students sat on the edge of their seats. They were all enjoying this. Picking on the pretty girl, made Fowler and the rest of her students heady with self-righteousness. She has gotten everything in life on account of her looks alone, they thought. And the class of rather unfortunate-looking people fancied that she must come from money too. The truth was Rella had nothing more. In fact, she probably had less than all of them.

"But, I don't understand. I didn't say anything about black people or any other ethnic group." Rella protested frantically.

Fowler pointed a think finger at her. "I said that if you continue you'll be asked to leave the room."

Some of the women behind her whispered euphemisms about the proverbial dumb but beautiful woman image, just loud enough for Rella to hear. Rella wasn't dumb; she was just innocent of the twisting and turning of words. Manipulation was not her forte'. She sat through the rest of class dumbfounded and was the first one out the door to escape the nasty looks. One of the other female students mutter "bitch" and another one followed her out of the classroom to inform her that she was a "handmaiden of the patriarchy."

Today was not her day. She didn't make it even half way to her car without a group of guys shouting vulgarities at her. They were young white frat boys trying very hard look like rappers and apparently act like rappers as well. They were still following only a few yards behind her when Rella opened her car door to spring inside, slam the door shut, and lock it.

Late 2001

The storm was still raging, but now it was engulfing everything. Rella had finally graduated last year and reality had informed that her degree meant nothing. She had moved to another state and a bigger city attempting to find a decent job but discovered since she was not related to anyone, she had no connections. Birmingham, Alabama was the type of city that loved its inbred upper-class and inbreeding in general. One does not need a college degree and experience, only a family tree that doesn't fork. A career was not in the cards for her. She was working for a temp agency that treated their employees like gaming tokens at an arcade.

Rella feed her two cats, watered the potted plant on her window seal and straightened up all her belongings. She had thought this through for some time. If I learn to play this game, if I really start to believe it's a 'dog eat dog' world then what kind of person will I be? She had asked herself this repeatedly. After the span of a year, Rella had come to a conclusion; but was not one she could accept. However, since she did not accept it, she could hardly survive in a world that demanded her acquiescence or perversion. I will not play the game, nor will I be kicked about, Rella told herself. She had an alternative solution.

Rella waited until it was dark and made a pot of chamomile tea. She left a note on her nightstand. Then left a message on Gwen's recorder when she knew she'd be busy at work and unable to hear the eerie calm in her voice. Gwen would take care of her cats. She had done her research and collected the right amount of sleeping pills. Cinderella then became Sleeping Beauty.

MY HYPATIA

Graduate school was nothing like the ideal I had naively envisioned; graduate school proved to be a perversion of Academia. I'd plan to settle into a field like I liked – a vocation for myself, that I could enjoy and pay the bills with as well. Well, that's if you consider teaching a vocation, and it just barely covers the expenses of life in the twenty-first century. My program was the Masters of English Literature at a university in another state from my alma mater, which I increasingly ached for the deeper into my studies I dove. Yes, I loved the subject matter, but the students and the faculty of Bolshevik University turned out to be potentially volatile and/or insufferable nutcases, many of whom were either on heavy medications (of both legal and illegal varieties), or should have been (of the legal variety).

The campus was not quite as old as that of the University of Tennessee at Chattanooga, but seemed older in the sense that it was poorly cared for. The brick streets dangerously uneven, as black mold and roaches infested every crack of the small town. Even the trees ached to be elsewhere. I had found very reasonable housing after amicably separating from my then husband, who proved to be a liar and thief after our divorce. My Spartan apartment was at the topmost of an old bricked Victorian of which the walls were layered with decades of ancient wallpaper. With the recent layers gone, the oldest layers peered out haphazardly. Much of the original paper seemed to have been inspired by William Morris tapestries; the flowering damask too faded in its reds, creams and yellows. Staring at the walls in my old apartment made me restless with the impulse to either peel off the rest of the paper from atop the damask or either left a nostalgic aching for an era I'd never seen. I hadn't much in the way of actual furniture, but old antiques rescued from the side of the road and many a thrift store. Books and odd coffee mugs and cat toys littered the corners of my small space in this anachronistic world, but it was mine and that was all that matter. I am not the kind of person who shares my personal space bubble well unless you are a feline or rabbit.

I preferred only a select group of fellow female students to converse with while on campus and had even a smaller number of friends that I considered to be close friends. Ironically, within my larger circle of acquaintances, most of these girls were of some not so popular Protestant Christian persuasion - usually not such a compatible match for a Witch...unless, you are in a place where anyone with any set of standards or virtues are harangued, then they can make the best of allies simply because they have to develop a concept of mutual respect and boundaries.

I did not intend to become embroiled in the social setting of a small university and declined invitations to such occasions: parties, organizations, or hallway gossip clubs. The latter proved to be the most prevalent, which is of no value whatsoever to the general good of humanity nor the personal growth of any individual. I recall walking to class in high boots and skinny jeans before the look was "in" in Alabama. Yes, silly females pointed and laughed as if they'd never left middle school. Two years later, they were dressing like me. Their adolescent behavior did not bother me; the fact that I was paying to attend a college that promoted such silliness enraged me. It should not be surprising that one could note the dumbest, most inane students, and yes, faculty as well, belonged to such unofficial gatherings of shit-slingers. I'm sure now that these students are out in the "real" world, looking back with chagrin at their behavior and praying to whatever god they may believe in that no one from Bolshevik University recalls their name and/or face.

And so, graduate school itself consisted of attending class, attempting to participate just enough for a good grade, saying hello to the select few individuals I deemed worth to acknowledge their existence, and ignoring the bad behavior of my peers and faculty as well as their attempts to lure others into their issues by juvenile behavior such as: openly jeering at another student in class, making childish faces at people (I'm not kidding), not doing their part within a group project, and slandering anyone who was actually attractive. Seriously, I paid to take classes at a graduate level with people who acted worse than kids I knew in middle school. I can say that their pettiness was a good distraction from the emotional pain of a divorce and worry for sickly loved ones; therefore, in a perverse way they did me a favor.

Being a Witch is not particularly easy or the safest form of spirituality to have, especially when you live in the American South. Sometimes the most avowed "open-minded" and "liberal" thinkers prove themselves to be among the most bigoted and narrow-minded. (Recall how they "loved" my boots?) I pretended to be something else entirely, and since I was not promiscuous, they believed it. Of course, one comes to the self-awareness that she is a Witch usually at a pretty early age when she realizes she has abilities and insights others do not. And no, I'm not referring to the magical powers of movie effects or television shows.

One afternoon, just like all afternoons during the week, I returned home from class. My apartment was just four blocks away from campus, and I enjoyed the walk in good weather. It was unseasonably warm for February, even this far South. The yard of the Victorian was long and wooded, the back completely encased by a brick wall hiding the overgrown garden of a back yard complete with bottle trees and an old, tarnished angel statue. I pushed the gate open, closing it softly behind myself. My cats mewed in the windows as I trotted up the gate, hefting my book bag over one shoulder. Once inside, I immediately locked my individual apartment door. I detest unlocked front doors. The evening proved to be uneventful: I fed my cats, made soup, washed dishes, readied for bed and read a couple of hours before falling to sleep.

I awoke around three in the early morning with the feeling of eyes on me; however, I was not alarmed. It was not the creepy feeling of unfamiliar eyes slithering across one's body; it was more of a presence. The garden that my bedroom overlooked lacked lighting other than the natural light of the moon that glistened silver on the treetops. I vaguely recalled that I'd shut the windows, knowing that the night would be a chilly one. One of my cats was perched on my chest staring at the space between the door and the chest of draws to the side of the door. The space in front of the tall, narrow chest was filled with a shape that was about the height of the piece of furniture, so I knew it was somewhat shorter than I; I'm half a head taller than the chest of doors. My cats did not seem alarmed, which meant I had no reason to be anxious at the nocturnal visitation. Yes, I'd seen paranormal activity that has been as real as any daytime event. I'm quite use to this; but, I did not expect the urgency that the being in front of me frantically tried to convey. She did not motion wildly with gestures but rather it emanated from her. She was slight of frame and by her shape I could tell that she was female. That was the only attribute definite about her other than she was opaque and very real. Transparency was not a quality with this entity. She was no "little ghost."

The concern for me that this being exuded was touching and disturbing all at once - what was she trying to tell me? She was visibly trying to warn me about something yet she did not want to scare me. And as I sat up to communicate, she simply stood there willing her sentiments at me with a wave of emotion without saying a word. Maybe she couldn't speak? She was dressed from head to toe in a black robed garment that hid everything about her but the shape of her form. Even her face was covered by an oval black cloth mask with an odd rim of white around it, almost like a nun's habit. I began to address her, and in response she slowly dissipated. I was left alone with a sense of impending danger and sadness. She'd made it very clear that I should tread lightly with the environment I'd found myself in: divorce, an antagonistic graduate problem, and I'd caught the attention of the one of the faculty – a dirty old man, at that.

The image of the figure standing at the foot of my bed stayed with me. I could not go back to sleep that night...I needed to speak with her. And I thought on her for weeks; and, as my personal issues became more intense before situations got better, she would find me again. This time, in a dream state....

...The girl skipped in the meadow below with her play mates. She was no longer a child, but definitely not a woman, somewhere in the twilight threshold of childhood and dawn of adulthood. She laughed as they chased down the meadow, her bonnet a nondescript medieval design, her dress brown. Her family was not wealthy but they were not entirely poor either. She received a little of an education, informally though. The girl cared nothing for reading boring scripture, besides the old women said it was unbecoming of a maid or matron to read. It could affect a woman physically, make her womb dry up, and

unable to bear children, then no man would want her. She had no idea what these old bats spoke about. And she gave no thought to the opposite sex other than her play mates who she played with in the meadows. If she hadn't have been such a tomboy, maybe she would have cared more about a formal education, but as far as she was concerned it was only the wealthy and clergy that read. And she certainly did not find either group impressive. Her life, the girl with ash colored hair and a sweet heart shaped faced, passed before me, images of her village, her time, and her death.

The ambience switched in a blink. Suddenly, the girl was the center of certain attentions. The older women of the villages watched after her predatorily, the other girls avoided her. She felt the change as though it was the wind. But she knew intuitively that it was something far more deadly than the wind, something feverish and insidious. Her water color eyes stayed wide in shock the last few days of her life. She had no understanding of how everything had suddenly changed. Was it the young man who wanted to marry her that she'd rejected? Or one of her mother's old, bitter friends. Maybe it was even one of the village girls who jeered her, calling out vulgarities whenever she ran errands for her mother in the market? Common society considered the girl to be very attractive, with smooth skin and pretty features with a sharpness but ripeness about them all at once. Sure, she preferred to be outside exploring the hedge of the village instead of sewing with the womenfolk. But she had never done anything to deserve the ostracizing and blatant ridicule of the village. The girl child was distraught with confusion. And then the priests came...

They arrived in the early afternoon. She'd missed lunch after strolling through the village on errands and had taken a detour in the pastures before skipping home. And when she did arrive home, she found her parents weeping and tugging at her, she saw them – the clergy. They did not look happy at all, but then men of the cloth never do. She felt a rise of panic in her throat. Who had died? was her first coherent thought. Her siblings were oddly absent. "Mother?" she questioned. Her mother only sobbed and screamed: "No, no, no!" The robed men rose, looking at each other uneasily. They patiently explained to her that she must come with them, that it was for her own safety. Confused and scared, she had been taught to fear and obey the clergy. But as she began to follow the robed men out of the rough framed door of her family's small but warm house, her father began to pull her back. That's when the village men, older patriarchs, grabbed her father and held him down as he struggled. The look on her father's peasant face scared her more than anything. It told her to be afraid.

One priest laid a gentle but firm hand on her shoulders. He was the younger one, and steered her away from the fast gathering of matrons and young maids alike. When she saw their faces she knew. The glares of outright hatred and jealousy explained everything as well as one word the hags shrieked: "Witch".

Terror exploded in her chest. No! There'd been some horrid mistake! She knew all too well what happened to witches. And she wasn't one! The young priest simply picked her up and put her in the barred carriage. She could hear the priests talking softly atop as the driver whipped the horses. She'd never ridden in a carriage before and certainly had not imaged it so bumpy. The carriage's wheels' seems to find every pot hole and land the wrong way on every cobblestone. She attempted to plead with the clergyman. They'd have to believe her.

She wanted to know why the woman had behaved that way. What had she done to them? They ignored her words, only throwing rotten food at the carriage bars.

The end of the carriage ride afforded her the night in the basement of the church. She was shut in a room with a lump of stale straw for a bed and a bowl of rancid water. Later the next day, the priests visited her in the cell. They questioned her about stuff she did not understand. She was not educated, nor was she inclined to philosophical thinking - she did not know how to respond. She understood nothing about their ramblings regarding the soul or damnation or any charges that village gossip had laid on her. She did witness the young priest argue bitterly with the old priest, and she cried for him to save her. He did not, and was not allowed to return. They, the ones in brown robes with metal devices, came to see her in the following days....

She was dehydrated, partially starved and only half conscious when they first shoved her into the stinging sunlight. She hadn't remembered the sun being that bright. A loud roar vibrated in her ears, making them ring. The only sounds she'd heard over the last couple weeks had been the trickling of basement condensation running down rock walls, the monotonous speaking of the robed men and her own screams. She had no clear recollection of a passage of time; she'd drifted in and out of a gray haze. They pulled on her wrists, which were blackish, the flesh worn to the bone in places. What was left her hair was thin and limp, her lips cracked from her own teeth as the flesh in other parts had been battered and torn. She did not understand the roar that was coming at her until individual faces registered in her thin memory. What had she ever done to these people?

Her eyesight had weakened and she squinted at the structure she was being hastily dragged toward. She lost her footing when the structure registered to her as a wood pile. One of the hooded men kicked her thighs to make her stand. The action only worsened her balance. A wail escaped her throat, as she struggled out of the instinctive urge to survive. One of the men grabbed the remainder of her hair, pulling her onto the small platform meant for her feet. She groaned as thin strands snapped, her necked popped in protest. The sack-like shift of a gown she'd been ordered to change from her peasant clothes to, hung in tatters around her emaciated form. The men tied her to the erected pillar and one began to read something. She searched the crowd frantically for a loved one to no avail. Then their faces registered, the individual people she barely knew, yet they were the cause of all her agony. Still yet they jeered her, contemptuously spouted defaming slander. She recognized unfortunate looking girls who had bullied her if they cornered her, older saggy faced hags, and young mothers.

She had come to understand over the past few weeks that malicious gossip, the wagging tongues of women, had condemned her to an even hideously organized Church, and a sentence only to be carried out by the men of their god. Never had she ever been given to notions of deep thought. God, the devil, religion, had not been part of her child world until now. Coughing, she cleared her voice. She did not hesitate to interrupt the priest's reading; she knew she was doomed. She had tried screaming out her innocence before only to be struck. This time she did not scream innocence. When she began to bellow out her words, the mob stilled: "I have done nothing to any of you and most of you I do not even know. But if you want me to be a Witch then a Witch I will be. I curse your bloodlines through eternity." The crowd roared once they absorbed the meaning of her words. The bonfire was lit as she raised her battered face to the sky and called down any so-called demon that would hear her. For a girl who had not entertained any philosophical thought of religious nature, she was ready to entertain the most unpopular notion of such at the hour of her death. And the demons who came for the hypocrites were actually avenging angels, as the girl was escorted her out of her mortal coil. **There are consequences to your past actions, readers dear. How's that karma? You know who you are.**

I tossed, must have tossed, a lot in my sleep as the bed sheets attested the next morning while I watched the flames in my nightmare began to lick the young girl. Suddenly after her words, I was seeing the nightmare from in her body – from her vantage point. I could see the ugly faces of old women and I knew why they wanted her to burn. And I was in her as she called out to the entities she naively called "demons." And I was there when she died, her essence exiting out of her body with a gush of wind as she swept upward through a tunnel of pulsating lights; the guardians answered her call. As beings of energy, they appeared as bright, primary colored green and red jelly fish-like beings of twisting forms. The reds and greens mutated into each other, blending themselves into the color of bile and puke, ready to humble the sanctimonious. We welcomed them and they fueled us, these beings of justice, karma, whatever terminology your consciousness can emotionally deal with.

After her death, I soared through the stratosphere crossing time as well as space. The mysterious figure was beside me again, her black dressings fully covering her body. I was simply wearing jeans, normal clothing for my era. She pointed to the Earth as we settled over a shopping center in my old home town. We alighted somehow inside the grocery store, she led the way down aisles as we glided through, unseen by very real, ordinary people. Everywhere I seemed to look I noticed discontent, mainly in the women. They were downtrodden and worn looking. One husband blatantly beat his wife in the face, tripping her in the frozen food section of a grocery store. She cried but there was no one else present on the aisle to witness his acts of violence. My guide seemed to enjoy the brutality. I was horrified by this at first. Where her spiritual presence alighted, chaos reigned. I exited to the parking lot to see more domestic squabbles. She was at once beside me, urgently wanting me to make some kind of connection that I couldn't.

"Why?" I asked. "How can you hurt them and want to help me? Why are you showing me all this?" I had known through the entire vision that I was "dreaming" – in an astral or lucid state. She knew I knew this and suddenly we were in nothing, around nothing, no where. Everything was a brilliant white room, except for the shorter female form dressed in black standing before me. And then she took off her mask.

It was the girl who had been brutally tortured and brunt in the village on the coast of Brittany sometime long ago in The Middle Ages. Her sweet face was flawless, and eyes clear. And I now knew everything I needed to know.

The next morning I did nothing, could do nothing, a heaviness had settled on me. I looked in the mirror to greet fair hair instead of my dark. I saw her face in place of mine own; I hung a towel over the mirror. That night she still haunted my reflection. The full length mirror on the back of my closet door shook with her image. I sunk to the floor weeping. Ages of tears rained out of us. Her palm touched my palm from the opposite side of the looking glass. Her blue eyes locked on my brown.

I know the reason behind it all and now I recognize who these people are, if not immediately then eventually. I found more of them just last year. And they are afraid of me, as they should be. I know who was in the crowd when they burnt her. We are both doing better know. I've graduated and moved on with my life, leaving a small town university quaking at the mention of my name. I gradually gave her a name; she didn't want her old one back.

As a lover of ancient histories and having worked in my fair share of libraries, I thought it only appropriate to call her Hypatia, after another real woman caught up in the misogyny of a bloody history and ultimately condemned and murdered by the same Catholic Church and cultural mentality that burnt my Hypatia. I will not pretend that my blood does not boil as I type these words, or that I have not been her. My own life time echoes an eerie similarity of verbal condemnation just as both my

Hypatia, as well as ancient Alexandria's Hypatia, faced.

My Hypatia showed me that they are all stone-throwers. And the proverbial "they" are simply the sheep that blindly follow the dogmatic and insular mentality of the Kool-Aid drinking masses. Ironically, both the self-extolled liberal communistic academics and the self-righteous religious zealots of any religious persuasion would have skinned Alexandria's Hypatia as well as lit the fire that burnt mine. In the gross vulgarity of their extremes, they are one and the same: a two-headed monster.

The last time I saw my Hypatia, she was standing at the foot of my bed playing with one of my cats. Her arms were bare in her sleek black dress, and her fair hair wrapped in a bun at the nap of her neck. She simply looked at me and smiled, nodding. Now she wants you to know her story.

MY (BEAN'S) VERSION OF "THE PUSS IN BOOTS"

I know the *real* Puss; in fact, he passed his vigilante duties onto me once while he was vacationing in the Gulf one season. (No, I did not wear those silly miniature cowboy boots Puss loved to stride around in on his back paws.) Puss had a fascination with bird watching in the tropics - at least this is what he claims to have been doing. I personally believe that he made his way down to the Mobile area all for that darling Turkish Van he had eyes for. I can just see old Puss now, chasing that young kit and her human companions across the cobbled streets of Fairhope, leaping through branches full of Spanish moss just to catch a glimpse of his beloved. But enough of that, this is a story about me: Senor Bambino Familiar (and maybe Vesper too).

I suppose I should describe myself: I am a well-proportioned, big-boned, orange tabby with amber eyes. I can melt you with my golden eyes if I need too. It's a special feline trait. Being of the tabby tribe, I have the proverbial "M" shape on my brow. Ladies of all types love me. My Mama (I should mention that she is human) calls me "pretty man" and I guess it's a fair description of me.

Anyway, back to my story. Old Puss comes tapping at the kitchen window one night. He's mighty impatient and I ignore him while finishing off my favorite treats. Eventually I jump onto the windowsill. I manage to push the window up higher from its cracked position by nudging myself through. (Mama hates it when I do this.) "Bean." He begins as I land onto the twilight lawn beside him. (A few select people call me just 'Bean'). "Son, it's time for ya to git some good trainin' in. I've got ta head further South for a spell."

He said this all so obviously rehearsed and all causal, gazing up at the purple martin's nest in the willow. I just had to pry. So I plopped down on the fresh-cut lawn and inquired just as causally, "Ol' Puss, what takes ya down yonder?"

"Me bones, young'un," he declares, dramatically stretching out with a grimace into the position that Mama inaccurately describes as "downward facing dog." I pretend to buy into his story for a while.

"Ya know humidity does an old tom good... I mean, boy, sometimes ya just got ta keep movin' at my age." He's shaking his head now in emphasis.

"What 'bout them birds? Tropical birds?" I widen my eyes, trying not to look suspicious. "And it's not humid enough here? Puss, we *are* in the Deep South."

Puss sniffs, looking at me out of the corner of his eyes, "It's that sea air that makes all the difference." His attention then focuses solely on a certain snob of a Turkish Van. My younger sisters do not get along with this Miss Van.

"Ah, I see," I announce a bit too loudly. "Her people have a beach house down there, ya know?"

Puss gives me a hard stare. "So you'll cover me?"

"Yessiree! I sure will," I replied. I didn't mind taking over the neighborhood watch briefly. It just went to the dogs if there wasn't someone to keep vigilance.

"Now Bean, it ain't gonna be no walk in the cotton patch this time. That devil dog is loose again." Puss looked at me squarely. I groaned. "I thought you took his eye?" Puss shook his head. "He's still got the other one, kiddo."

The following week Puss was off on his trek and I was the Alpha in town. No dog caused any problems the first week. The only thing to report was a big nasty garden spider who flat out refused to move her web from the porch of Granny Muffet's cottage. We'd had problems with that man-eater before. That spider kept her web right over Granny's rocking chair until one morning she lost her balance and fell right into Granny's oatmeal. And ya know what Granny did? She ate that spider just out of spite. It did give Granny Muffet quite a bad case of constipation. At least that's what she told Mama the following evening very expressively from across the yard.

One morning, during my second week of duty, Vesper had to give me her two-cent's worth. "So you're taking over Puss' place." It was said as an observation, not necessarily a question.

Now Vesper Woolf is my much older and often anal sister. Puss reminds everyone that she is older than he, much to Vesper's agitation. We are often reminded that Vesper is from a long line of Woolfs. And no, I'm not talking about the lupine kind either. Woolf as in Virginia, if that rings a bell to ya. Yes, Vesper, a tortoise-shell tabby is somehow a direct descendant. Anyway, this is what she and Mama run around telling people.

We sat on the veranda overlooking the copse of willow trees to the side of the house. She'd been there most of the morning watching the sun creep over the line of trees in the distance.

After taking my time I responded, "Why yes, Vesper, I am. Puss stopped by himself before his vacation and bestowed this distinct honor onto me." I always try to sound pompous around Vesper since it's her natural state.

Vesper snorted and started to clean behind her ears with a gray paw. "Bean, your bloated ego never ceases to surprise me. It's quite annoying but also morbidly entertaining as well." She was trying to sound bored with her fake grating British accent.

"Well, Ms. Woolf, at least I'm of a clean genealogy free of pompous embellishment." I received a stinging bite right on the left haunch for that remark before I made it down the steps.

I did see the girl with the red jacket skipping down our pebbled street. She lives a couple of fields over on one of the horse farms. This pleasant kid takes our road to the bench at the end where that big orange monstrosity full of other noisy human offspring stops. I follow her out of boredom and for the occasional treat she'll sometimes pull out of her pocket for me. This day she has me a treat; I sit with her on the bench and eat my piece of sandwich meat while she rubs my back. The early morning sun rises on our bench with the dew still sparkling in the grass until that noise maker turns the bend and starts roaring its way toward us. This is when I always jump down, trotting into the thicket watching her and trying to understand why she gets on that thing with all those obnoxious brats.

As the monstrosity pulls away, I spy that dog – the big black with just one good eye – in the field across the road. I stay still and silent wondering what on earth he's up to. He's just sniffing the ground and digging in the same spot. It couldn't have been a rodent. No rodent would stay close enough to the surface to allow itself to be caught. He continues to dig and sniff not once even taking a crap as his actions suggest. Dogs are so stupid. I started back to my porch, bored with spying on a one-eyed dog.

Later that evening I reported in for dinner and was fussed at for being out and about all day. I passed by Vesper perched on her favorite spot on the sofa. "Thought you were too busy saving the world and that I might get your serving," she purred, just slightly opening her eyes.

"Nope, just the neighborhood. So sorry to disappoint by showing up for dinner," I responded, smirking.

Vesper wheezed slightly. She swallowed the hairball instead of spitting it out. That meant she wasn't too cranky. "Where did those two kits run off too?"

"Upstairs in bed with Mama," I replied.

Vesper sniffed, "Figures – little shits." She has yet to refer to our two recently acquired baby sisters by their names. It takes Ms. Woolf a good while to warm up to anybody. Most people never get in her good graces. "You know, that little fat one always eats everyone's leftovers." Vesper flicked her tail with her comment.

I sat on the stairs eye level across from her. "If we had bigger bowls…"

Vesper interrupted, "Yeah, and if a frog had wings he wouldn't bump his ass every time it hit the ground either.

I decided to give up on making small talk with Vesper and found the blanket in my basket freshly fluffed. That night I slept pretty good.

The next morning was the same old routine. I wondered exactly what it was that Puss did with his time. He refused to adopt him a human family, but Mama and Granny Muffet always put some food out for him. Granny referred to Puss as "a barn cat." He was never too impressed with this assessment. Mama thinks he fathered our two newest additions, but Puss won't talk about that subject. Vesper doesn't like him. Puss claims it's because she's "fixed" or something. Says I am to but that I've somehow managed to maintain my character. Once I asked Vesper what he meant by all this and she swatted me upside the back of the head. She says Puss is just a strung-out old tom and that if he were a human male, he would be one that drinks lots of smelly liquid and makes gaseous sounds and smells.

I thought the rest of this day would continue to be full of lazy musings and vivid daydreams until I heard the shriek of a human cub. I bounded out of the shade of willows to the edge of our yard. It was that big black dog trotting after my girl with the red jacket. Vesper yowled something at me from the porch as I leapt down the pebbled road. That giant dog must have had some nerve because he didn't pay me so much as a glance. Instead, he reached out and grabbed the girl's jacket, pulling her roughly down onto her backside. I was on his back in that instance. He yelped as I used his back as a scratching post. The dog dropped to the ground and rolled over as I scrambled to escape his girth. I sprinted back to the willow trees. The girl with her tattered red jacket scrabbled all the way to Granny's door. Granny Muffet, stumbling on her long dark skirt, stepped out onto the porch with her fire stick and aimed right at that dog. However, she missed and the dog ran off. I didn't have to climb a tree after all.

Mama was running toward me. She didn't let me out of the house for the rest of the week. I tried to explain to her how important it was for me to carry on Puss's duty, but she ignored me.

"It won't do any good," Vesper explained. "I've told her for years that green is not her color yet she still insists on wearing it. Hell, the damn walls in here are green!" I pouted as Vesper continued her rant about artificial green colors.

It was a few nights later when that dog showed up at our kitchen window. Vesper woke me with a sharp tap on the shoulder. "Get up!" she growled lowly. I uncurled groaning and opened my eyes to not only Vesper but the kittens staring at me too.

"What is it?" I stepped reluctantly out of my warm basket. Mama was breathing softly on the bed. We could tell she was asleep by the pattern of her breath.

The kittens started to mewl softly. "Shut-up! Get back up there." Vesper swatted them away from us. "If you don't get back into bed now I'm going to rip into you both." The girls hurriedly climbed back next to Mama. "Now stay there or I'll eat you for an early breakfast." I was yawning as she turned her attention back onto me. "Come on, butt breath. You have to see this." So I followed her down the stairs to the kitchen window where Puss and I often chat.

I paused. "Well?"

"Well, look out the damn window!" Vesper jerked her head toward the sill.

Wanting desperately to return to my basket, I compiled. With a hiss, I jumped right back down. "He's just staring at us!"

"No shit, Sherlock. You're the one he's insisting on speaking with," Vesper informed me dispassionately.

"How do you know *that*?" I asked.

"He told me so," Vesper responded in a tone that implied I was incredibly dumb.

"You mean you spoke with *him*?" I was taken back by the idea of Vesper conversing with any stranger, much less a dog.

"Yeah, I did." She crept back onto the windowsill. This was one time I was elated to see the window closed. I followed her, not wanting to look like a coward.

"Good evening." I begin, trying to deepen my voice. Then I noticed that this beast wasn't scary at all, just pathetic. His one good eye watered and his paws where messy.

"Okay, he's here. Now what do you want?" Vesper demanded, swooshing her tail.

"I wasn't going to harm the kid. I'm just looking for my bean seed. I thought she'd taken it." He was pathetic and a bit loopy.

"That's it...that's what you wanted to tell us?" Vesper was about to launch into one of her rants. I tapped her paw slightly and turned back to the dog.

"Why do ya need a bean seed? Are you a vegetarian dog? I thought they were all extinct along with the unicorns," I asked.

Vesper rolled her eyes. "More importantly, why would you think the human girl would have taken your bean seed?"

The sad dog sighed and flopped down to the ground. "I heard her mention something about a bean then the martin in her willow explained to me yesterday that he's Bean – I mean, not a bean but called Bean. I feel like such as idiot."

Vesper laughed. I glared at her. Turning back to the dog I explained, "Yes, I'm Bean, it's short for Senor Bambino Familiar."

"Wow. That's a really big and important sounding name," the dog responded. I started to puff out my ginger chest and say something smart when Vesper had to start in about her name. It was my turn to roll my eyes.

"So," I interrupted. "Where could you have lost that bean seed? And do explain again just why you need a bean seed?"

The dog sighed. "Not just any old seed, this particular kind of bean seed. You see, it makes a very special bean sprout. One that goes all the way to the sky – that's where I'm from."

Vesper and I both found ourselves at a loss for words. She was the first to respond. "You know what I saw the other day?" She said to the dog.

"What?" He seemed to perk up.

"A fairy! An annoyingly pink fairy taking a shit in my litter box!" Vesper's voiced was playfully spiteful.

The poor dog was transfixed. "Really? What did you do?"

Vesper grinned, exposing all her fangs. "I ate that little bitch."

The dog gasped. "Vesper, please...she's not serious," I told the dog. "She just tells bad jokes."

The poor creature began to whimper. "I just want to go home...please help me find my bean seed!"

I sighed. "Okay, I'll see what I can do. Where else could you have put that bean seed? There's plenty of fields around here."

"It disappeared. I know where I put it and it's not there! Someone has stolen it!" The dog sounded a bit crazed.

Vesper had a suggestion regarding the fate of the bean seed. "Were any birds around, especially crows? They love to dig up seeds. I hate those little moth...."

I cut her off again. "Look it's nearing dawn and I want to nap before breakfast. Get some rest and I'll see you in the morning about your bean seed."

"Oh, thank you!" The dog didn't look as sad after I promised to help him. And sure enough, he was waiting for me at the edge of our lawn the next morning.

"You're actually leaving the house?" I was surprised that Vesper would consider trailing along.

"Why I wouldn't miss this for an extra bowl of salmon treats. Bean looking for a magical bean seed with some one-eyed, homeless dog." Vesper was downright gleeful.

"Good morning," I greeted the dog cautiously. He was still a dog no matter how pathetic he may be.

"You can call me Jack." He yawned. "I didn't sleep too well at all. I miss my bed."

Vesper spoke up from behind. "Well, Jack it's semi-pleasant to see you again. By the way, what happened to your other eye?"

I turned around and glared at her. "This was going so well..."

"It's okay...I was born blind in one eye," he said absently.

"Really?" Vesper pushed past me. "Blind in one eye from birth?"

"Yeah. It's not as bad as it looks." The dog yawned again.

Vesper turned to me and whispered, "I told you that washed-up old puss of a tom cat was full of shit."

I would have come up with a sassy retort if Granny Muffet hadn't of stepped out onto her porch and given the three of us a weird look. "Hey! Hey! Ya'll won't believe what's happened to me again!" she shouted in her cracking voice across the yawn.

I looked around, "I think she's talking to us. There's not a human around – she's talking to us." The dog began to whine.

"I know ya'll can understand me. I ain't dumb to that stuff." She continued, "Come on over here so I don't have to shout it out to the entire Southeast."

"Of course she's speaking to us," Vesper snapped and began to walk toward the old woman's front porch. I followed closely as Jack crept behind timidly. Vesper stopped on the first step. She tilted her head up at the old granny and meowed.

Granny Muffet shook her gaunt face, "I'm constipated again. Yep. Ate something I shouldn't have." She looked at me and winked.

"The bean seed!" I turned to Vesper. "She ate Jack's bean seed."

Jack began to whine. "Don't worry, old boy. I'm gonna give it back. Ya see I took some laxatives this morning and when they kick in...."

"I really don't need to hear this." Vesper started back to the house. Turning to look back over her shoulder she said to me, "Looks like the mystery of the magical bean seed has been solved. Too bad the old hag didn't let it sprout out her ass. Now that would have been one for the story book."

Yes, Granny Muffet did make sure to pass her bowel movement in the meadow behind her house conveniently fenced in by trees. No, none of us were present to witness this. No more than two days later, there was the most ungodly sight Mama said she'd ever seen – a gigantic bean vine growing straight up into the sky. It was about five tree trunks thick and its end couldn't be seen for the white clouds that gathered overhead thickly that week. The last we saw of Jack the one-eyed black dog he was clumsily climbing that giant bean sprout, wagging his tail at all of us in farewell.

"But, big brother Bean, where did he go?" Morgana the little beauty looked up from Puss's old boot. It would fit her paw in a couple months.

"Well, no one knows for sure. Ya know Granny got out there and chopped that beanstalk down, raving something about a giant," I replied to the big orange orbs gazing up in awe at my story.

Luna, leaned up against me, "Mama said that that dog climbed all the way to heaven," She explained in her tiny voice. Vesper was right – Luna was quite chubby. I didn't say anything about that though. I just put my paw around her healthy neck and gave her a nuzzle. I replied, "That sounds about right to me."

THE WICKED BITCH OF THE SOUTH

The smell of turpentine was too strong the day she woke up. Turpentine and something else – something slightly rotten. She realized it was her own flesh. How long? How long had she been sleeping? It had all been an out of body experience – too Twin Peakish to be real. The pain in her chest, the searing ache in her gut, told her otherwise. Angie got up and took a shower.

She scrubbed everywhere and still felt the oppressive weight threatening to overwhelm her. Her own conscience ate at her. Somehow *she* felt like she was the culprit, but then all victims feel so. How? How could she have let it get this out of hand? Stupid …stupid …stupid …it grew into a mantra in her head. She gripped her long dark hair, tugging it hard. She suddenly knew when it had begun.

She had not had a long courtship with Chester, but then they had cut right to the chase and been completely open. Married after five years, they both mutually had decided to have a child, a baby girl and a wanted child. Nevertheless, *his* family, his evil family, had been on their ass to "get pregnant" since their first day of marriage. Chester was the exception to his family, or so she had thought. He was an example of a child turning out the exact opposite of his family. He had waited until after they were engaged to introduce Angie to them for fear of scaring her off. After all, he was from a family of all boys where the common notion of a female equaled incubator. However, his mother was responsible for this notion rather than his father. This is often a petty irony.

The first few years were so natural, so contented. They thought it would be wonderful to have a creation of both of them. And so, Alice was born. She promised to have the darker genes of both her parents, so it took them a bit off guard when Chester's mother, Delilah, decided Alice would be her favored grandchild. Delilah was as tan as she burn herself, and as blond as she could bleach with muted light eyes that she attempted to pass off as violet. Her girth was one of a cartoon prima donna; she fancied herself one as well. Delilah was a bitter, wrinkled shell of a "had been." Her family's origins were of a ruddy German stock, which secretly Angie was glad Chester hadn't inherited any of the physical traits. She much preferred the Cherokee.

Alice was also the only female grandchild in a family that exalted males. Immediately Delilah began to interject herself into the Wood's family life. It begin was her bringing gifts and escalated to her throwing tantrums that would better suite an adolescent girl in high school than an aging baby-boomer. For the first time, Angie and Chester began to fight.

She sat twirling her paintbrush in a glob of algae green. Raising an eyebrow, Angie thought she mixed in too much linen seed oil. My life is too damp, she thought, the pervading dampness must go. She raised her eye level to the scene beyond the porch of their trailer. All this had been a very bad idea. The pond with its cattails and its green scum enthralled her for some reason. It was beautiful to her, and what so many in passing would call a swamp. My entire life is a wetland, mildewed with might-have-beens and good intentions gone awry. She almost wished to herself but stopped. Chester was standing at the other end of the rickety porch glaring at the space of water as if he could glare it into non-existence. He was not a water sign and irrationally afraid of snakes.

Chester was almost too big for the tin roof that rested just half a foot above his head. "We don't have a good reason, we just don't." His words came out too forced. He had to spit them.

"After everything she did. Everything she said. Everything she did too you as a child, you want that bitch watching your daughter?" Her voice quavered. She couldn't help it. This was *her* baby, goddammit, not that fat high-class whore's. She'd pushed Alice out; she was the one who had ripped open, a crimson tide surging out of her, not Chester. He'd heard it all and it was starting not to register. Chester cared too much about people who really did not care that much about him. He was a typical human male – dumb to the intuition and needs of his mate. She realized that she hated him.

"We have plenty of reason!" Angie hissed.

"Passive-aggressive womanish bullshit will not hold up in a court of law, Angie!" His voice sounded loud but hoarse. He bought his hands down hard on the rail in front of him. He spoke softly, "I've got to think of my father."

Angie knocked the canvas off her easel as she stood. Arching her back like her cat, she hissed "Your father doesn't give a flyin' fuck about you!" (She almost regretted the words as soon as she spoke them – almost.) "You're not his Jacob, you're Esau! What has he ever done for you that he has done for your perfect Nazi brothers? You, the spitting image of his yesteryears, are his least favorite. You! We live in a trailer – a doublewide trailer and your parents are multi-millionaires! Your brother drives a Mercedes! You betraying me, who stands beside you through the light and dark, for a family that doesn't know how to love, only collect material wealth!" Her nostrils flared at him.

Chester stood stunned for a moment then launched into a tirade. He had an atrocious temper that flared then died. When he was done he flopped into the lawn chair behind him. Angie picked up her canvas and sat it back on the easel. She found that she could no longer paint.

"The bitch is threatening to sue," he said softly. "She's a socialite with a bloated ego and a rich man's money. She's going to sue for rights to our child – 'grandparents rights!'"

Angie snorted. "Whoever heard of such an asinine farce of an accusation?!"

"They're a block vote, a block hunk of the population – fucking boomers; she will find sympathizers." Her husband already sounded defeated.

"Tell them, tell everyone about your childhood, about her." Something urged her to jump into the pond right then. She might hide among the plankton and cattails.

"There is no proof. No tangible, factual, witnessed proof. They'll say it's all in my head, all just 'middle kid syndrome.'" Chester sounded like he was already defeated.

By the time the case of "grandparent's rights" was brought up in the Atlanta Courts, Alice was nearing six. She was precocious in awareness for her age. Alice was the silent child who would observe the other children on the playground from her swing like a hawk regarding sparrows. Her movements were sure-footed and precise, her eyes slightly tilted like her father's though they had her mother's sharpness. Alice did not miss the woman observing her out of the corner of her eyes. She took care not to look directly at her. That would make the woman think that she was actually acknowledging her. She sat on her swing, moving her skinny legs slightly with the breeze and observing out of the corner of her eye like a bird of prey.

She could feel the blond woman's eyes one her dark braids. They were long and thick. Her mother called them "her glory." The woman eyed them. This made Alice nervous. She would cut them if she got the chance. The thought surged through her mind. She knew who this woman was. She'd met her before always bearing toys, but first demanding a hug. Alice could only remember seeing her twice, maybe three times. She knew her mother did not like the woman who was her grandmother. Neither did her father. Just then a boy - it was Tyler - chased a ball out into the grass. This gave Alice a chance to follow him with her line of vision and a better, yet still discreet, view of the pink blond woman.

She was with two women that much resembled her. Their faces were drawn and soft and hair shortly cropped. Not beauty, Alice thought to herself. What was the sour-looking pink lady thinking? Alice felt her stomach churn.

Alice was so engrossed in finger painting that she didn't notice the women approaching. One was her teacher who had a strained look on her face and the other was the pink blond, with her friend sporting short-cropped hair. Alice swooshed her fingers in the cup of water and dried them off diligently on the paper towel beside her. The other children seemed to be engrossed in their own artwork. She searched the room and found only Tyler's eyes met hers. His eyes were big and dark. Her teacher sat down across from her. "Alice," she began ever so tentatively, "today you will be going with your grandmother."

"I am not allowed to," Alice answered matter-of-factly.

At this the pinkish woman dropped down to her knees (with much effort) and grasping Alice by the arm, Delilah spoke, "I finally get to show you the room I've kept for you." She was not prepared for the response that came.

Alice met her stare. "Do not touch me. I do not like dolls. Why would I want to play house when I'm meant to be an astronaut?" The girl's eyes were as dark as her son's. Delilah for once was speechless.

The pink woman looked to her teacher for support but Mrs. Slayton did not acknowledge her. Alice could tell that her teacher did not like this at all.

"Alice, I am your grandmother, your father's mother and I want to get to know you. I love you." The pink lady stammered out the last sentence.

Alice met her gaze, slitting her eyes like a cat. Delilah reluctantly thought that *her* grandchild looked faintly Indian. "How can you love me and hate my mother when I came out of her?" Alice was young but knew how to use a rhetorical question. The pink lady was speechless and Alice thought she saw her teacher's lips curve up a bit.

Her grandmother's thin lips lined even more into a horizontal line. "I have a court order that says I get you for the night and tomorrow. Do you understand that?"

"I understand that you are a bitch," Alice responded just as matter-of-factly. Mrs. Slayton turned her face away from them. Alice thought she saw her teacher shake slightly. Tyler's mouth was now slightly open, his eyes still big. The woman's companion mumbled something about "the child being warped." Alice glared at her.

"Are you a man?" she asked the woman with the short-cropped hair.

They had to haul her out of the classroom kicking and screaming. The other children were transfixed. Mrs. Slayton refused to help them pull her out the door. She and the man-looking woman exchanged a few strained words. Her parents were in the hallway but held back by men in dark uniforms.

Her mother's eyes were bigger than normal. She looked terrifically beautiful, her hair a weedy mass like an enraged mermaid. She knew her mother would be crazed. She was more surprised by her father. He used words on the pink lady who had been his mother that she had not heard before. The woman who had been his mother did not care. She thought she was getting what she had always wanted – a daughter of her own. She was wrong.

Once in the pink woman's oversized vehicle, the other two women left them alone. She had explained to Alice that they were there for "moral support." Alice had decided that it the best course of action would be to ignore the woman and seem indifferent. After all, the woman talked and talked so that she couldn't keep up with her. Alice thought of what her Daddy always said about "prattling" women; he was used to her mama's intense silences.

The pink woman talked about everything and anything. Alice could not follow her changing subjects. "I'll show you Jesus...I go to this wonderful church...we'll go out to eat...I want Italian...kids like Italian...do you know Jesus? Why on Earth would Chester let her name you Alice?...you look like a little papoose...(Here the woman reached out to touch her braid. Alice leaned into the car door.)...you would look so pretty with shorter, high-lighted hair...what do you think?"

"I think I'd look like a tramp. Little girls shouldn't be dolled up like big girls." Alice glared at her. This woman was insane. She'd talk of religion and hair-styles simultaneously. The pink woman was quieted for a moment. She did not have a rebuttal for Alice's common sense. Alice was insulted regarding her long locks and the fact that this woman, who wanted to be her grandmother, considered her a doll.

They pulled into a large parking lot outside of a big building. The woman got out of the car and opened Alice's door. "Out we go." Alice could tell that she was trying to sound cheery. She would not hold hands with her, instead walking a little behind.

Inside the big store the woman found the girl's section and showed her a bunch of incredibly fancy dresses with frills and ruffles. They reminded Alice of the outfits little girls wore in fuzzy old black and white photos.

"Try them on," the woman urged.

"I am not a doll." Alice stood emotionless.

The woman got mad and flew into a tangent about how ungrateful Alice was and her daddy too. "You two will never appreciate anything. And your mother encourages it." She spat the word mother out.

Alice's eyes darkened even more. "We don't like stuff like this. It's silly."

This time the pink woman responded to her common sense. "Do you not ever think for yourself? Can you not pick out what you like?" Her voice was shrill and sharp. She thought she was making a point.

"Did you ever let your children pick out what they wanted? Even when they are all grew up?" Alice replied in her singsong child's voice.

The woman glared at her. "We're not going until you try at least two of these on. You've got to have something to wear to church."

"I don't go to church."

"You're going to start going with me. Everyone needs to go to church."

"How do you know that's what everyone needs?" Alice blinked up at the woman.

"I don't - Jesus does." The woman's mouth closed into a thin line again.

"How do you know what this Jesus guy wants?" Alice asked thoroughly engrossed in the conversation now. Her grandmother looked astounded.

"What do you mean 'Jesus guy'? Have you no idea who He is?" She seemed unsettled but at the same time happy, as though she'd gotten something she needed.

Alice felt that everything depended on what she was going to say next. "I know about all that...it's my parent's business to educate me on that stuff, not yours."

The woman rolled the words around in her head as if she were examining them for dirt. Alice couldn't tell what she thought for a moment. "Well, you need to be exposed to Christianity. I'm a Christian and Jesus had helped me through..."

"Is he Mexican?" Alice's voice was purposefully purely inquisitive.

This stunned the pink woman. "What do you mean?" she asked weakly.

"Jesus sounds like a Mexican name. Is he Mexican?" Alice's eyes were black coals, reflecting back the star-lit stares of a long-forgotten race.

The woman licked her lips. "Well, in the Presbyterian faith...I don't know! Here we're buying this one!" She angrily held up a fluffy pink dress.

"I don't like pink," Alice said looking the dress over like one would inspect a pile of vomit.

The woman in pink, herself, seethed. "You'll like it! You'll like it and you'll wear it!"

They went to more stores in the mall and to a restaurant. Alice did not eat much and her father's mother carried on about how she must have gotten her mother's frame then accused her of being anorexic.

"What's that?" Alice was too young to understand much of what this woman said.

The woman told her things about her daddy when he was little. Alice asked for stories, but the woman only made absent comments. "You look like him, you know. It's around the eyes and brow line. You have those same hooded eyes." Her grandmother studied her now and her eyes actually grew moist. "They're not my eyes though," she observed. Alice touched her own forehead, feeling her brooding brows.

The woman sitting across from her changed like a fall breeze. Her mouth formed a hard line again. "Unfortunately, you're going to have your mother's nose. That's why you need to work on your femininity now because with a hawked nose and brooding eyes no one will see your beauty." Alice had no idea where the conversation had gone. She blinked in confusion.

"Your cheekbones and waistline will not redeem you. Men don't like white women who look... ethnic." The woman dressed in pink sat her glass down with a clink and smiled as if she were letting Alice in on a secret. Alice remained confused.

The woman who was her grandmother lived in a gigantic house. "There's a room all for you," she said to Alice, leading her up the stone steps. The rooms were enormous. The kitchen was half the size of her home.

Inside was her grandpa. Alice knew him. He came by to visit from time to time but she had no idea he actually lived with this woman. He patted her head companionably and asked if she'd liked any of those dresses her grandmother had picked out for her.

"No," she replied honestly.

He laughed, "I wouldn't either."

Her grandmother sighed at him and told him not to encourage her. They watched a movie with a pretty, blond cartoon girl and afterward the woman announced it was bedtime. Alice knew this was the moment.

"I want to go home...I want my kitty."

"There are plenty of stuff animals here that you can sleep with." Her grandmother reassured her.

"No, I mean my real life kitty, GraySkin."

The woman gasped. "You sleep with an animal?!" To her grandpa she said, "Can you believe that! A baby sleeping with one of those filthy animals!" Grandpa didn't seem to hear her. He was listening to a man on TV talk.

"SHE IS NOT FILTHY!" Alice shouted.

"Don't raise your voice to me!" The woman's face grew to a deep shade of pink.

"I want my Mama! I want to go home!" Alice was crying now. She'd acted like a little adult all day, and found she could not hold up to the task anymore.

"You're not going home. You're going upstairs right now to bed. Tomorrow is a big day. We're having lunch with some people who I want you to know."

Alice kicked and screamed. She threw a tantrum right there on the den floor. Grandpa told her grandmother to just take her home. She would not. Finally, he picked her up, spanked her and carried her upstairs. Alice screamed through the door the same words she'd heard her father use earlier that day.

She waited. She waited until the house grew still and opened the bedroom door ever so slowly. She crept like GraySkin down the stairs. She could see a faint light coming from the direction of the den and the muted voices on the television. The door will not be locked, Alice thought to herself. She opened it as soft as she could and stepped out onto the stone steps.

Her sneakers made little noise as she padded down the lawn and out onto the street. Alice walked for what seemed an eternity to a little girl alone in the dark. In her childhood naiveté, she thought her home could not be far from here. Alice continued to walk into the bright lights and the widening road.

The police did find one little blue sneaker. There was no trace of the child. After a year, Alice was pronounced dead.

THE DYING AGE: A LOVE STORY

I knew you when the old chaise lounge had just started to fray around the corners, thin threads of tapestry roses bleed in single strings onto the fading rug. An era is coming to a close; the guard changing. Sunlight filters in through the lace curtains, dappling the wall, that old green damask. I imagine rabbit heads and fluffy bottoms poking out of the floral swirls, their noses twitched in anticipation of what your next words would be to me, as I stood in my house slippers and that long blue gown. The pine floor needed waxing; I needed an embrace. Here we were; here we are. Time is an illusion...so they say in the time of moon landings and talking boxes. To me, time always slows here, in this ever-fading room. The pink roses on my gown grow paler with each return to this memory. You are still just sitting in that high-backed chair. They, those in the future, will say it looks like "the Mad Hatter's" chair with its red violet velvet and embellished filigree frame. Now the chair is just the fashion, a quickly dissipating fashion as the door closes on this Time. Is time not real? If so, then why do you always feel so real then...just as you do now? And how is it I remember that olive green vest you preferred, the brass pocket watch you would snap shut with finality? Somewhere, someone has a picture of us like this, from this time. Somewhere, long ago I left my contentment. I think

I left it at this moment in this room. And now there is only this....

The estate is not far from the cliffs; I do not bother with my boots, those buttoning black ones that go so well with the silky petty coats you pester me to wear. Nothing is as it should be, as it should have been. This impending doom always bent down on my shoulders and neck, like your horrid heritage. Could you not just have been you? I'm the only one to ever have known you, truly to have seen who you are? There are no walls, only the ones in our minds. The hedge rows grab the end of my gown as I stumble along the field. The broom is growing high and soon its yellow flowers will haunt this landscape for another season. "Rosemary, thyme, and sage...." I sing quietly, just that one line. Everything is not going to be fine.

I will cry for you as I hit the rocks, those flat, wide blue stones at the end of the shore. I tumbled down the jagged edge of the cliff; it was not a clean fall. As the cliff ripped at me, I felt warm and sticky. I think I may have wailed.

You enter the darkened room; my window overlooks the sea. I tell you that one day I will have to return, that you really shouldn't call me your Selkie. You laugh; you've brought up a decanter of sherry from the pantry. I look at my face in the looking glass, the elaborate one in black iron. Sometimes my own reflection scares me. You always tell me not to be silly, such things are signs of hysteria. I always tell you my fears. You do not always tell me yours. You hold them inside that stoic brain, never letting in the weak need to open. And because of this, you are the flower that never bloomed.

And of all things, it is this epiphany that hits me as my body strikes the earth.

1997

Men are Poison.

They eat fresh young girls.

He killed my desire;

My heart bleeds.

A man can decay a woman like green rot.

He haunts the Dark;

His demonic god devoured my universe.

He hasn't a shred of Grace....

Now home is here.

My Angel Cat smiles;

The Broken Cat laughs.

Our ghosts hear all.

They know about the magic.

Life is an ocean of yesterdays.

1998

They try to sculpt and chisel us.

The free are dead.

You know which "ism" did this....

Live life as a metaphor and feel pain.

He makes her suffer – if only she were hard like me.

He is Dust here.

I am always angry;

Some think too bold, but never empty.

I am naked with secrets in my fiery mess of passion,

There is no joy – only demand.

Life is a mad song.

My angel of Sex and Death says we are glass.

I can break.

AFTERWARD

I am a translucent woman, a bone white silhouette
of thought.

You had only a latex heart as a god of black holes.

You know there is no cosmic plan, only a litter-box
of salt and stardust.

I picture you like a broken coffee cup, yellowed
porcelain and dirty.

You are no longer young sex candy between my
pillows and teeth,

But a lost destiny.

I dreamt of fiery red hair,

An Angel in corduroy that haunts my life.

My self-effacing love is an empty symbol of us.

DISAPPOINTMENT

My entire life has been a black hole of dreams gone wrong.

I've rode Queen Mab's night mare for too long.

Learning how to overcome you, your race, your hate.

My Kind lives across an ocean of stars,

And no messages can be sent in quaint, little jars.

As I live this mortal life, I die in mortal strife only to recall

The Tall Ones as they were when they ruled this plane,

Leaving it to humankind, now to their regret and shame.

You feel the true origin of my soul, as you should.

I would not change your fate if I could.

FROM BEAN TO MOGEEN

(Note: Mogeen rhymes with Bean. In other words, the "Es" are long vowels.)

Once upon a time in a cozy kingdom lived a big-boned tabby cat, who claimed he was not flabby or fat. His name was Bean, short for Senor Bambino Familiar, but his eyes were not green.

Bean's older sister, Vesper Woolf, was quite lean and her eyes were green. When he would sit on her for a laugh, Vesbie would get quite testy and exclaim, "Oh, Bean, don't be so mean!"

Morgana, the princess of all cats, was definitely not a bit fat. Her people hailed her Lady Mogeen and oh did she preen!

Luna had a bit of a belly but it didn't jelly quite like Bean's. She was somewhat lazy but that's because she was born half crazy.

Sometimes Bean would suck in his gut and strut around the den. Old Vesbie, drunk on her catnip gin, would giggle as Bean's belly tried to wiggle, "Bean! Bean! Jelly Bean!"

Mogeen was not keen on Bean's prancing. She was the one to be dancing! "I am the beauty! Vanity is my duty!"

Vesper would wail, "Go stick your head in the garbage pail, you little brat!" Mogeen would then shout, "At least I don't have the tail of a rat!" and trot off to pout.

Luna loved her sister quite dearly because Mogeen could be rather sweet. But Old Vesbie was right Mogeen could be fearlessly trite, especially when Bean would eat all their treats.

Vesbie! Bean! Lulu! And Mogeen! Their Mommy would sing. Dinnertime the clock did chime and all four kitties were served each a dish of delicious fish.

Luna would cry to be fed first and Mommy did try to quiet her slightly retarded baby girl. Then a riot was started and in all the excitement Bean farted. Vesper departed demanding, "Feed me over here!" As Mogeen darted about everywhere singing, "Bean! Bean! Smelly Bean!"

GABRIEL

The fallen Angel you were, the Vixen I am...

As the Golden One, you fell hard and I tried to save you...

But I only had long locks of inky black and you rejected that.

We could have made the Stars fall instead, but the possibility of "us" only made the other Angels jealous.

Pride was our sin as we descended into the Abyss of human folly: Maybe some melodies are better left unsung? Maybe some books are better left unwritten? Maybe our children are better left unborn?

And what would have happened if we created our own race? The Demons would rage and the Seas would roll.

I am falling, falling like the Nephilim. I swam like the dolphin, but burned like The Maid. Yes, I burned...I am still burning for you - my Shemjaza. And I did look for you to saving... but you were saving someone else instead.

And I burn, and I burn, and i burn and i burn and i burn and i burn and i burn and i burn....I now know that you never really loved me.

CHANGELING

"Serendipity," pronounced The Owl.

"Nevermore," quoth the Raven.

Both were overruled by The Cat:

"Does not matter because you are all mad here."

The Cat continued to purr.

"If she wasn't mad, then she wouldn't have come here."

"She's another haunted Beauty, once loved only to be forgotten," appraised The Owl.

"Unicorn Fated."

"Maybe she is just out of her pocket of Time?" the Cat mused.

The Serpent uncoiled herself out of the universal sea.

"You all belong to me because I am the only one who unconditionally loves you."

MORGANA LE FAY'S BLESSING

The ultimate power is not caring about what others think of you....

When I feel alone, I know that this is just a place for solitude and introspection.

When I am unfairly judged, I stand tall and hold to my convictions.

When I am sad or angry, I know that this will pass.

When I am told that I am not smart or gifted, I know that this is spoken out of spite.

When I am told that I am no beauty, I know that this is spoken out of jealousy.

When I am met with manipulation, I blind it with the light of honesty.

When I am met with adversity, I am firm with grace.

When I find myself in despair, I recall all the blessings of my life.

WE

Like a Neverending Story, we circulate through the
stratosphere,

Never quite ending, but somehow we forgot The
Beginning.

You love me for a day; I loath you for a second.
And then we make love.

Always a Constant, always a Dream.

A Northern Star I am to your Setting Sun.

A thunderstorm you are to my rain.

Never, yet always, I am your woman.

ABOUT THE AUTHOR

Amber LaShea Geislinger lives with her physicist husband and furry children somewhere below the Mason-Dixon Line. She plays the harp, crafts pendants out of pressed flowers and vintage paper, volunteers for cat and domestic bunny rescue non-profits, and is a defender of feral cat rights. Geislinger is a M.A. of English Literature. Her alma mater is The University of Tennessee at Chattanooga.

www.ingramcontent.com/pod-product-compliance
Lightning Source LLC
Chambersburg PA
CBHW061214170626
46809CB00003B/1350

* 9 780615 710792 *